# Who Needs a Boyfriend at Christmas?

## Betting on Christmas

### Delancey Stewart

# Contents

# Chapter One

## Zane

The highway flew beneath my tires as I headed for home.

*Home.* It was a funny word, one people used so casually to describe a place they belonged.

For me, it didn't hold much meaning. Holly Creek was a place I'd never really belonged—not that I'd figured out yet if I belonged anywhere.

The bike roared beneath me, the unending vibration and driving wind filling my body and head, making the action of traveling into a visceral exercise that succeeded in distracting me from the potential of what I'd find when I finally arrived. I'd been on the road for three days, and the motorcycle had begun to feel like another appendage, or really, more like a funda-mental part of my body. An organ, vital for life. I wasn't sure what would happen when I reached my destination, when I stepped away from the machine, when I was once again just Zane Crosby.

The Holly Creek hospital wasn't huge, but it was one of those glassy shined-up buildings that made you feel like maybe you should have changed your clothes before stepping inside.

And the moment I moved through the doors that slid open with a gentle whoosh, I wished for a few more days on the road.

A bright and chipper brunette beamed at me as I entered, as if she didn't notice the grimy leathers, the three-day scruff, or the tattoos that snaked from beneath the collar of my jacket and up one side of my neck. I swallowed hard against the antiseptic scent of the hospital lobby.

"Can I help you?"

"Yeah, uh..." I reminded myself to maintain eye contact. I'd found over the years that people responded better if I didn't regress to my naturally aloof nature, if I smiled a little, if I engaged. But it was hard today. After three full days of zero human interaction beyond the occasional nod to the people working at the gas stations where I'd fueled up and the managers at the dingy hotels where I'd crashed, I felt even more removed from humanity than normal. "I'm looking for Ben Crosby."

"Patient?"

"Yes ma'am." I shuffled my helmet to my other arm and forced myself to keep a pleasant look on my face. "My father."

She glanced up from the computer she'd been staring at while her fingers flew over the keys beneath the counter between us, a soft expression filling her dark eyes. Then she returned her gaze to the screen for a moment.

"Three ten. Just take the elevator over there and when you get to the third floor, make a right. The nurse's station will be just to your right, and they can help you from there." She pointed to the bank of elevators.

"Thank you." I moved away, relief seeping through me at the break in pleasantries, even as trepidation filled me over the thought of what I might find in room three ten.

One more polite interaction, this time with a gruff male nurse whose name tag said Ezra, and I was standing in the doorway of room three ten. There, tucked beneath a green blanket, asleep, was Dad. His body was outlined by the blanket, a narrow form that was nothing like the intimidating hulk of my childhood memories, nothing like the terrifying figure of my teenaged years. Dad was an old man. Feeble and sick.

And somehow that made it worse.

I stepped into the room, fighting some kind of emotion I did not recognize. Dad and I had never gotten along. We didn't like each other. But I was all he had, and so I'd gotten the call.

I wouldn't have come, except for a promise I'd made my mother before she died. Looking at the frail old man before me now, that knowledge felt vulgar somehow. What was there to be afraid of? To be angry about?

I moved across the room, setting my helmet on a table and zipping off the leather jacket to drape across the back of a chair. I sat next to Dad's side and let out a long breath.

"Hi Dad."

Dad's head rolled toward me, and one eye popped open, the iris within shining in that same dark brown hue he'd passed on to me. "Zane."

I nodded once.

"You came." The words were simple, but the tone expressed something like surprise. And maybe even wonder.

"Yeah."

He squeezed his eyes shut tight for a moment and alarm flared within me. I was used to anger and intimidation from this man, but the simple expression on his face was much closer to tears than anything else. I wasn't sure I could handle his emotion. Not when I'd steeled myself for years against every-thing else.

"I'm glad," he said, and that harsh voice was soft, full of something like gratitude. "Thank you."

My lips pressed themselves together as my head spun. I didn't have words for this situation. Instead of speaking, I lifted a hand that felt like lead, and dropped it onto his, noticing how bony and frail he'd become.

We sat like that for the better part of an hour, and Dad seemed to drift back to sleep. After a while, the beeps and hums of the machines had lulled me into something close to sleep too, and I was startled by the entrance of a doctor.

"Hello," she said, her scrubs and official nature leaving me no questions about her role here. "You must be..."

"Zane," I supplied, standing to face her. "Ben's son."

A smile flickered across her serious face. "Glad you could come."

"He okay?"

She offered a curt nod, and then smiled at Dad, who'd woken to watch this interaction.

"Your dad's had a pretty rough time. The heart attack was fairly serious, and we did an angioplasty to help open the arteries affected. This clearly wasn't his first heart attack." She was looking at the tablet she carried as she said this, but my head snapped to Dad. He'd had other heart attacks?

The doctor continued. "Between the general weakness and the advancing dementia, we'll just need to be sure that Ben gets the support he needs when he leaves the hospital. We have resources that can help you."

"Dementia?" My head spun. Dad was turning seventy this year, and I probably spoke to him twice a year on the phone. I'd been gone more than a decade; I guessed it wasn't a shock that a lot could change in that time.

The doctor continued. "I've talked with Ben a bit about his living situation. It may be time to move him somewhere he can get a little help."

I turned my gaze to Dad. An old folks' home? Was that what Dad wanted?

"Retirement communities have come a long way," the doctor was saying. "And Ben and our staff have discussed a number of options. I'll leave it to the two of you to make some decisions, but we have liaisons on staff who can help with the process."

I nodded, stunned. "Thanks."

The doctor left and Dad stared at me through watery eyes as I came to grips with this new version of the man who'd filled my youth with a constant, overwhelming presence. That man was gone, I realized. He'd been reduced by age and sickness... and so what did that mean for us? If I wasn't afraid of my father, I wasn't quite sure what to be.

"We'll figure it out," I told him, sensing that the frail old man in the bed at my side needed my reassurance. "I'll figure it out."

Dad closed his eyes again and slept.

# Chapter Two

## Sabrina

"You made me move into a Gothic mausoleum and then you abandoned me here." I pretend-whined, my phone pressed to my ear while I walked home from work. The day had been so nice, I'd decided that my little purple truck could have the evening off. It was only a couple miles.

"Sabby." Chelsea's voice took on that be-reasonable lilt she used when I ventured too far into the realm of exaggeration, which I had a habit of doing. "It's an old Tudor-style house, not a mausoleum. And I didn't abandon you. I moved in with Rex."

"I know. And I'm so happy for you—"

"Which is why you've agreed to be in the wedding." Chelsea practically squealed this interruption.

"Don't make me change my mind."

"Don't say that! Rex's mom would freak. She's very controlling. The numbers have to be even!"

"I would really hate to disappoint Mrs. Buchanan." I did not give a rat's you-know-what about Mrs. Buchanan. But I loved Chelsea.

"You say that with sarcasm because you only met her once at the engagement party, and she was on her best behavior. She's

6

terrifying." Chelsea actually did sound frightened. How bad could Rex's mom be?

"Anyway, she's not my problem. My problem is the empty bedroom and the looming rent payment for September."

"Sabrina, I hate to say this, but that's exactly why I paid for the whole month of August. To give you time to find someone." I hated it when my best friend's voice turned all teacherly.

"I tried."

"Mentioning to three people that you might, sort of, need a roommate is not considered really trying."

"Maybe not," I admitted miserably. The truth was that I'd enjoyed having the place to myself, even if it was too big and potentially haunted. "But I need to actually try now. In a hurry."

"Put up signs at work?"

"Yeah. I should."

"Craig's List?"

"No thanks."

"Yeah, that could get creepy."

"I'll figure it out. Go have sex."

Chelsea actually giggled and something inside me winced. It wasn't that I wasn't happy for her, because I was. And Rex was great. It was more that I knew it was unlikely I'd ever find a guy like Rex for myself. And I was getting to a point where I didn't actually feel like I needed one. Most of the time, at least.

But as I hung up with Chelsea and let myself into the big quiet house at the edge of Holly Creek's little downtown district, an encompassing loneliness swept through me, even as the warmth and familiarity of home greeted me. It *was* home. But it was still empty. And quiet.

"I like quiet," I reminded myself. I'd moved to Holly Creek after school, partially to escape my enormous, smothering family. Quiet was good. It had been the point. Mostly.

But I still needed a roommate to help with rent. I owned the coffee shop downtown, but between keeping the lights on there and paying my employees, plus recently replacing the coffee machine, and saving up to open a second location, I wasn't exactly swimming in spare funds.

I'd need to actually look for a roommate.

Tomorrow.

For now, I was going to pour a big glass of wine, find some cheese and crackers, and plant myself right in the middle of the couch to start *Ted Lasso* over for the thirtieth time.

# Chapter Three

## Sabrina

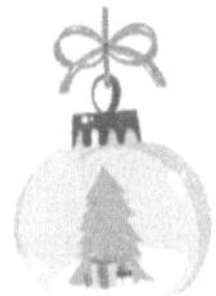

"Hey Sabrina, a girl asked about the flier while you were on break." Paul handed me a folded piece of paper as he moved from the register to the coffee machine to pull an espresso. He'd worked here since I'd opened Brewed Awakening, and was the best barista I'd ever seen. Watching him work was like going to the ballet, or witnessing a perfectly executed Olympic dive, or seeing confetti stream out of your cousin's piñata that you were supposed to let the kids bust open but accidentally destroyed with one light swing of a golf club (I'd probably never live down the shame of stealing a kid's birthday joy.) Maybe not that last one, actually. That one was just me.

"Thanks," I said, unfolding the paper, which had the name "Ally" penned neatly across the top with a phone number and a little heart at the bottom. I sighed. I'd had a lot of interest, which was good. But this was exactly why I'd put off replacing Chelsea so long. I knew finding someone I could tolerate living with was going to be a challenge. Chelsea was perfect. She was kind and outgoing, but she also managed to be away from the house most of the time, and that gave me plenty of what I loved—alone time.

"How long you gonna leave those signs up?" Paul asked. He knew as well as I did that a week—at least a week in which I'd had a lot of interest—was probably long enough. I just needed to choose someone.

"I don't know. I need to get someone in ahead of September's rent. But how do I choose from names and phone numbers?"

Paul delivered the drink he'd made and returned to stand behind the counter, frowning at me. He crossed his arms over his chest and I had the sense he was formulating words, so I waited. Paul was what people called the strong and silent type. He was friendly, but didn't go out of his way to be social, and he had a championship resting bitch face that tended to make people wary. But I knew the guy was a teddy bear.

"Those phone numbers... you could like, call people."

I cringed. I hated talking on the phone. Especially with strangers. "Ew. How will I figure anything out on the phone?" I'd be too busy worrying about what to say next.

"Just call to invite them to interviews," he said finally. "Tonight."

"Interviews? It's not a job," I pointed out.

"Living with you?" he said, his eyebrows climbing toward his short dark blond hair. The sarcasm was clear in his tone, and I whacked him on the chest with the rag I'd been holding to wipe the counters.

"Ha." I thought about it. "Yeah, that's a good idea. Just suck it up and get them done in one fell swoop."

"I'll hold down the fort. And give you the thumbs up or thumbs down so you have some extra input. Just do it at that table." He pointed to the little table closest to the counter. "And talk loud."

So it was decided. And that evening, I positioned myself at

the little table and greeted the first of four people I was interviewing for the job of roommate. Housemate, really.

A bubbly blonde named Trina came first. She wore very high heels, a very short skirt, and enough foundation to spackle the tabletop, were there any reason to do so. Her voice was high pitched, and her laugh was higher. She earned two thumbs down from Paul and sapped most of the enthusiasm I had for the interview process, and a little of my will to live.

The next candidate was a woman named Lesley. She was straightforward and practical, clear about what she was looking for and what her expectations were. A little older than me, and something in her expression told me she'd seen more than she should have in the years she'd lived. I liked her fine, but Paul's vote was lukewarm. Sideways thumb.

Erika was next. A college student with a clear enjoyment of all things marijuana related. I had no problem with that in general, but I didn't like the idea of smoking in my house, so she was a no for me, though Paul gave her another sideways thumb and asked her for a connection as she left.

The final candidate was Ally, who was my leading choice despite the heart on her note because she seemed generally normal and easy to get along with. But she had cats. Three of them.

"I'll let you know what I decide," I told her, walking her out.

"No cat ladies," Paul said, leaning over the counter on his forearms and shaking his head. "It could be catching." He put out his arm, turning his thumb down.

"Well thanks a lot for nothing," I said, turning back to him with exhaustion weighting my limbs and something like desperation bubbling at the back of my brain. "Really, any of these could work. It's not like I have to fall in love with a roommate. Just live with them."

A customer had come in behind me as I'd headed back to the counter, and when I rounded it, joining Paul at the register, the guy strode towards us. He had spiky dark hair and a square jaw that I thought could probably cut glass. He was tall and strong looking, with muscled arms that made his black T-shirt pull tight around the tattoos on his biceps. He swaggered to the counter holding a motorcycle helmet and carrying a leather jacket, in jeans that hugged his hips and thighs. Something about him suggested darkness, danger.

I was immediately attracted.

Because of course I was.

"Can I help you?" I asked, consciously reminding myself that guys who looked like trouble were usually trouble.

"Yeah," he said, his voice a leathery rumble that made my stomach swoop. "Large Americano." He pulled a wallet from the back of his jeans, and I worked not to be mesmerized by the way he moved—like some kind of lethal assassin or a predatory big cat zeroing in on prey.

I managed to ring him up and hand him his coffee without embarrassing myself—my specialty where hot men were concerned—and then turned away from the counter instead of staring at him as he left.

Only, he didn't leave. He wandered to the bulletin board by the door, sipping his coffee and scanning the fliers hanging there. When he saw the one I'd put up looking for a roommate, he pulled it down and read it, his face solemn in concentration. After a moment, he turned back toward the counter and approached, holding the flier out.

"This says to inquire at the counter."

Paul stepped close, an eyebrow raised. "You're looking for a place?"

"This your ad?" The guy asked back.

"Maybe." Paul pulled himself taller, like he was preparing to defend my honor.

I elbowed him, shaking my head. "No, it's mine."

"Tell me about the place. It's near downtown?" The guy put

the flier on the counter and fixed me in his dark gaze, sending my blood rushing around inside me, heating all the while.

"Uh, sure. So it's an old Tudor-style house. Two bedrooms, both pretty big, with a shared bathroom upstairs. A kitchen, living room, and dining room downstairs. On the edge of downtown."

He nodded. "Rent?"

"Six hundred?" I had the distinct impression he was interviewing me. I cleared my throat and tried to take charge. This was my house, dammit. "First and last for deposit. No smoking, no cats."

"No problem."

"How soon are you looking to move in, ah . . . sir?" I asked.

"It's Zane. And as soon as possible." He rubbed a hand over his jaw, and if I hadn't been certain he was trying to convince me that he should get the spot, I'd have interpreted his expression as disappointment. "Month-to-month lease, though."

Paul made a coughing noise and I glanced over at him to see both his thumbs pointing down in a very not-subtle no-vote.

"Um... yeah, okay."

Paul sighed and Zane frowned at him, then returned his intense gaze to me.

It kind of felt decided. Like this guy, Zane, had basically just interviewed me and accepted me for the job of his roommate. Dammit, this was all backwards. I needed to take charge.

"Do you have like... references?" I knew this was probably not the right roommate, but I felt a little desperate after the evening's blah interviews, and something in me besides my raging attraction to the guy was telling me that he might be a good fit. Despite the somewhat intimidating outer packaging.

"Yeah. Can I share a couple contacts?" He held out his phone.

"Oh, uh, okay." Very modern. Here, I'd been planning to write them down. I entered my number into his phone and a moment later, he'd shared three contacts.

"You can call them all tonight. Jonathan works for me back in Denver. The second one is Eddie—we've been buddies for five years or so." When I frowned at the thought of using a "buddy" as a reference, he added quickly. "Character reference."

"Okay."

"Last one is my last roommate. Rebecca."

"You always live with the ladies?" Paul asked, stepping close again and doing that glower he probably thought was intimidating.

Paul was big, but when it came to intimidation tactics, he could learn a lot from the guy standing across the counter.

"No," Zane said, meeting Paul's gaze with a shrug. "They tend to be cleaner and quieter."

The guy spoke my love language. "I'll just give Rebecca a quick call," I said. "Can I let you know tomorrow?"

He looked uncertain for a moment. "Wanna call her now?"

"Why you in such a hurry, mate?" Paul asked. "In some kind of trouble?"

"You find that a lot of people in some kind of trouble are eager to fork over eighteen hundred dollars on the spot?" Zane returned.

"Just sayin'." Paul shrugged.

"Just got into town. Need to stay a while. Don't see any point in paying for a hotel room if this is a fit."

I was dialing the number he'd given me and stepping into the back to make the call, but as soon as I was through the door I had to pop back out. "Hey, what's your last name?"

"Crosby," the guy said, cementing my belief that he was the most attractive man I'd ever met. Zane Crosby. What a perfect name.

Rebecca sealed the deal. She gushed over Zane's meticulous nature, his consideration, and his tendency to do unnecessary chores like cleaning the refrigerator or making sure her favorite apples were always in the fruit bowl. "I miss him," she said, sounding wistful. "We only lived together for a year, but he was great. He ended up buying this ridiculous loft downtown and didn't need me anymore."

"And were you guys, uh..." I wasn't sure why I felt the need to ask about their relationship status.

"Dating?" She laughed. "No. I kind of wished, though. Zane is great. But he's a total loner. Friendly and kind, but kept to himself in that department."

"Aha," I said, having discovered nothing to warrant the word. Maybe Zane wasn't into women. Not that it mattered to any part of me except the silly lady parts that had decided to fire into action upon his arrival after months of dormancy. "Well, thanks."

"Yeah," she answered. "Glad he's found a place. It's gonna be hard for him, being back home."

"Oh?"

"Yeah," she went on. "With his dad and everything. I'm sure he'll tell you."

Huh. So Zane was from Holly Creek. The idea that he had grown up here cemented my decision. "Thanks, Rebecca."

I stepped back out to the front of the shop to find Zane and Paul still facing off over the counter. I had the sense that Paul thought they were locked in some kind of silent stand off, but Zane seemed to be simply waiting for me to return, his demeanor calm and steady.

"She pretty much raved about you as a roommate," I told him.

A tiny smile lifted one side of Zane's lips, which were thin but sculpted. The dark eyes flashed. "She's a great person."

"Well, I guess that's it," I said, unsure how to proceed. "When would you like to move in? I just need to find someone before rent is due for September."

"How's tonight?" Zane did not appear to be joking. He pulled the wallet from his pocket again and began counting hundred-dollar bills onto the countertop between us.

Paul said, "Why are you walking around with so much cash?"

Zane stopped counting and looked across the counter at Paul, patience radiating calmly from his expression. "I was hoping to find accommodations as quickly as possible, and wanted to be able to secure a place when I found it."

"Oh." Paul still seemed put out, but I poked him and we exchanged a look in which I told him to back off and his look apologized before he relaxed a little.

"I've just got an hour here to close up," I told Zane. "I can meet you there if you want to go get your stuff."

Zane gave me a quick nod, and turned toward the door before spinning on his heel to face me again. "Your name?"

"I'm Sabrina," I told him.

"Thanks, Sabrina. I'll see you in an hour."

# Chapter Four

## Zane

I would have gone to Dad's, but there was the pesky requirement of a key, which I did not have. And I didn't have the best memories of leaving that place anyway.

I needed a place to crash.

I needed something easy and temporary.

And I needed it right now.

Not the best combination of requirements for the diligent house hunter. Luckily, I was not house hunting. I was literally bed-seeking, and the bed I wanted needed to be quiet and empty, and free of complications.

Sabrina's ad had promised most of that:

*Furnished bedroom in charming house. You'd share with a quiet, polite, non-smoking roommate and no pets. Inquire at the counter.*

I couldn't have cared less that the house was charming. The rest of the ad promised exactly what I needed.

Sabrina, on the other hand, was pretty much exactly what I

generally tried to avoid. She was small, curvy, and just veering enough into alternative territory that she would have gotten my attention anywhere, not just because she happened to possess the room I needed.

She wore her hair short, and it was dyed a vibrant shade of blue, while her eyes were fringed with dark lashes and stood out in an equally startling hue of green. Her skin was pale and smooth, and there were a few charming freckles skittering across her nose, and a swan tattoo on the inside of one forearm. When she spoke, her voice was a husky, smoky thing, stirring up something inside me that was better left sleeping.

Sabrina was sexy and self-assured.

And none of that mattered. I would regard her as my house mate only. Until my dad recovered and I could go back to Denver. End of story.

I wandered downtown for an hour and then waited in the coffee shop until Sabrina and the silent glaring guy she worked with finished cleaning up behind the counter. I helped them stack the chairs on the tables, and headed out the door with them as they switched off all the lights and locked up. Were they dating, maybe? It was hard to figure out the situation, but the guy shadowed her like an overprotective Doberman.

Good. Knowing she was spoken for made everything easier.

"Want to just, um, follow?" Sabrina asked, tilting her head to one side as we stood in the warm pool of light beneath the streetlamp overhead. The air was warm, but it was the kind of warmth that was laced with gasps of brisk chill—Fall doing its best to take hold after the long steamy summer had held it down too long.

"Sure," I said, strapping on my helmet.

"I'm the purple pickup truck," she said, pointing to a garish truck parked at the edge of the little parking lot next to the store.

I suppressed a smile I hoped she couldn't see beneath my

helmet and Sabrina and Paul headed for the parking lot. He didn't live there too, did he? I guessed I should have asked a few more questions. Not that it would matter.

Still, I was relieved when they parted ways in the parking lot. No hug, no kiss... so not dating, then. Interesting.

I followed the little purple truck through the sleepy downtown side streets. Holly Creek wasn't a big town, and the concept of downtown was different than in a place like Manhattan or Denver. It was quaint rather than urban. With a town square, and family-owned businesses lining the streets. Dad's shop was on the edge of the downtown area, and the apartment I'd grown up in was above the shop. We passed both as I followed Sabrina home, and I let my eyes scan the plate glass window out front, the rolled-down garage door at its side. It looked exactly as it had my whole life. Maybe a little grimier.

The sign—*Crosby Metalworks*—was still in place, though it looked like the light over it had long since burned out. I swallowed hard, as if I could swallow down the rise of emotion seeing the place again brought back.

After just a few moments, Sabrina turned in next to a two-story Tudor house that sat a little way back from the street behind wide flower beds that were overflowing with blooms. A huge tree with sweeping branches stood to one side of the front yard, and a brick path led to the purple door from the sidewalk.

It was cute.

A little off-brand for me, but it didn't matter, since the situation was temporary.

I parked at the curb and walked to where Sabrina had parked her car to one side of the house. There was a little garage behind her front bumper.

"You don't park in the garage?"

"The owner uses it for storage," she told me. "Come on, I'll show you around and get your key and everything."

We entered through a back door, which I found myself

disappointed to discover was not purple. We stepped into a small but functional and clean kitchen, counters shining under the overhead light Sabrina flipped on. As soon as we stepped inside, a comforting scent wrapped around me. It held layers of something sweet and an undertone of some cleaning product— not like the sterile scent of the hospital. This smelled homey, lived-in, and my chest pulled a little. I remembered the feeling from being a kid, visiting friends' houses. What my own house had smelled like maybe, when Mom was there.

"Kitchen, obviously," Sabrina said waving an arm like a game show hostess presenting the prize I might win. "Pantry here." She opened and closed a door too quickly for me to get a good look inside. "We can share dry goods like flour and sugar, but you've got your own shelves in there for everything else. Same with the fridge."

"Okay." I followed her through an arched doorway into a room with a wooden table in the center, an ornate chandelier dangling over it.

"Formal dining room. For all the dinner parties you'll be having." She threw a grin over her shoulder and met my eyes, and for a second, my body tried to revolt. She was gorgeous, and her half-nervous demeanor made me want to reassure her. Or kiss her.

Dammit. I was not going to kiss her.

"Probably not a lot of those in my future," I told her.

She turned fully to face me, the smile still lighting up those startling eyes. "Okay, well, the option's here if you need it."

My hand itched to reach out, to touch her.

"This is the living room," she said, guiding me into a large room at the front of the house. The front door was through a small entryway, and the stairs climbed a wall opposite it. "And up here," she said, beckoning me to follow her up the stairs. "Is your room."

This last bit was delivered as we climbed the stairs, but I

barely heard it because Sabrina's ass was swaying back and forth at eye level as we climbed the stairs. Damn, she was sexy.

"That's my room," she said, pointing down the hall.

"Bathroom here," she flipped on a light as she passed the bathroom, and I glanced inside. Functional. Bigger than I would have thought. "And you're here."

The room she waved me into was perfect. Gray walls, a white duvet on the bed and a desk and chair in the corner.

"The closet's not huge," she said, pulling open the sliding wooden door. "And there's a dresser here." She gestured to a low, long piece of furniture with drawers. There was a mirror hanging above it, and I caught a glimpse of myself and managed to shoot a hard look at my reflection. I was here for a purpose, and letting myself become attracted to Sabrina was not it.

"Think this will work?" she asked me, turning to face me in the center of the fluffy rug that lay on the floor of my new room.

"This is perfect," I assured her. "I should probably let you know, I don't plan to be in town long. A month or two. Just here until my dad recovers."

Her smile dropped a bit. "That might have been nice to know a little earlier," she said. I could see that she was thinking about having to find another roommate again soon.

"I'll pay a few months' rent when I leave. To make it easier on you. I just really appreciate the space," I said, kicking myself mentally. Why was I giving away money I really didn't have? She hadn't even asked. I didn't owe her anything.

But when Sabrina's smile lifted again, I felt like I'd won some kind of contest.

I cleared my throat and looked away. Better to avoid any entanglements that might confuse matters.

No matter how attractive she was, no matter how much I might want to pursue her if the circumstances of my life were different, I needed to remember why I was here. Get Dad as healthy as possible, get his business sorted so he could get back to work, and get out of town. Though... seeing the man so frail and depleted, and the use of that word, *dementia*... the plan was potentially going to have to change from what I'd initially imagined.

"All right," I said stiffly, angling my head at the door in a silent suggestion that we were done here.

"Oh. Right." Sabrina turned to leave. "Um. Good night, Zane."

I watched her walk out of my room and shut the door behind her, doing my best not to replay her journey up the stairs ahead of me as I closed my eyes to sleep that night.

I failed.

# Chapter Five

## Sabrina

That first night at home with Zane just down the hall was odd. I'd become used to Chelsea's quiet late-night habits—the running of hot water into the bath, the final trip to the kitchen for her tea, finally the quiet click of her bedroom door. There'd been something soothing about her routine because in a way, it had become my routine.

But Zane? Zane was silent. He'd said goodnight, run a quick shower, and I hadn't heard another thing. I had a big family, and in my experience, women were generally quieter around the house than men. True of my mother and father too. But Zane was working hard to shatter my preconceptions. The man was some kind of hot, tattooed ninja.

I woke the next morning unsure if he had already left or if he'd simply pulled his door shut and might still be sleeping—silently, of course.

Not that it mattered in the least. I had a life and work, and didn't need to focus too much attention on the sleeping habits of my new roommate.

I opened the shop at five, and put in a full day. Half of it was at the counter, where I really enjoyed chatting and pulling coffees for the townspeople of Holly Creek, who were mostly friends at this point. The second half was paperwork, for which I shut myself into the small office at the back of the shop and struggled to reconcile the accounts. It wasn't that there was anything really wrong at the heart of the business. I always struggled with this part, but I didn't care what pundits said—anyone could run a successful business, even if math was about as difficult as alchemy for some of us. That's what computers (and accountants) were for. Overall, Brewed Awakening did very well. Not like buy-a-yacht-tomorrow money, but that had never really been my goal.

All I wanted out of life was to stand on my own two feet. To take care of myself and make my own way. And that's what I was doing. And soon, I hoped, I'd have a second location to show for my hard work. And then? I wanted to see the world.

I wanted other things too, if I was honest with myself, but I had begun to accept that I wasn't the girl those other things were for. I was the sidekick, the cute friend. Chelsea finding Rex had just been the latest example of me playing the fun friend to the smoking hot blonde all the men competed for. It had pretty much always been that way, and I was finally old enough that I could accept it. My life was fantastic as it was. And it was enough.

Later, once the doors were locked and the last customer had gotten their drinks and snacks, Paul and I locked up and turned toward the Tap Meister Brewery at the far end of the square. We stepped inside to find Anya—my best friend since moving to town six years earlier—sitting at a little round-topped table, sipping a glass of white wine. When she spotted us, she put the glass down carefully and grinned, her dark eyes gleaming.

"Hey, you guys!" she called, rising as we approached.

"Anya!" I gave her a big hug and inhaled her familiar scent. I swear she still used Love's Baby Soft perfume, and managed to make it smell sexy and modern even though I was pretty sure it was a throwback from the eighties. She had a secret stash somewhere.

"Paul," she said, hugging our tall, stern friend.

We all sat, and she told us which starters she'd ordered, as if we would be surprised somehow that our Thursday night ritual was exactly the same as it had been every Thursday for the past couple years. The only thing that had changed in our pre-weekend get together was Chelsea's absence.

"So..." Anya said, leaning in once we'd gotten our drinks. "This wedding. Dresses hideous?" Anya was invited, but she wasn't going to be a bridesmaid like me.

"No, actually," I said, sipping my wheat beer. "I like mine. Color, fabric, length, all good."

"Darn," Anya pouted. "I was hoping for drama. The only drama I get anymore is when Alex steps on a Lego brick or when Charlie asks for juice and then refuses to drink juice and acts like I've offended him by getting him what he asked for." Anya's life was dominated by the cutest toddler on the planet, Charlie, and her wife Alex.

"I try really hard not to do drama," I reminded her.

Paul snorted.

"Something to say?" Anya asked him, raising an eyebrow and giving him her attention.

"She lies," he said simply, narrowing his gaze my way.

"I don't lie!" I definitely did not lie.

"You just signed up for a whole spare roomful of drama," he said, and Anya's head swiveled to look at me.

"What's this? Roommate?"

"Yes," I said, making room for the tempura mushrooms that were being set down in the center of our little table. "I found a roommate. That's all."

Paul snorted again.

"What?" I asked him. "Clearly you have an opinion here, so go ahead and try using your words." How had he worked with me all day and not said anything? If anyone liked drama, it was Paul, and he'd clearly hung on to his opinion to bring here for Anya to enjoy.

Paul stuffed a mushroom into his mouth and made us wait while he chewed and finally swallowed, washing it down with a sip of his beer. "Well," he began, taking far too long to utter that one measly word. "Sabby here has given her spare room to a leather-wearing, spiky-haired, tattooed gentleman with piercing eyes and a voice that probably melts the clothes right off most women."

Anya clapped her hands and bounced on her stool, turning to me. "What? Who's this? Why don't I know this?"

"You do know. Big-mouth Paul just told you. And I didn't pick the guy for his looks." I waited for the lightning to strike after my little white lie, but was relieved when the scent of ozone remained blessedly absent.

"More. Tell me everything."

"That's basically all I know," I said.

"So he is hot?" Anya asked.

"I didn't say that. Paul did." I glared at the traitor who was eating another mushroom.

"Paul, something you want to tell us about your preferences?" Anya asked him, grinning.

He remained unfazed, wiping his mouth with his napkin. "I like the ladies. But a man who is assured in his own masculinity has no problem acknowledging when another man is attractive. And this one is. Plus, get the name. Zane."

Her eyebrows rose. "Zane. Like Zane Crosby?"

My gaze snapped to hers. "You know him?"

She blew out a breath and leaned against the back of her stool. "He was in my high school class." Anya had grown up in Holly Creek. "Total hottie. Loner, though. Had this whole tortured hero thing happening."

"Huh." I thought about that. It was pretty much an exact

match for the guy living in my guest room, even if he hadn't told me as much.

"Word was that he left right after high school. He and his father were supposed to run the business together, but they had some kind of falling out or something, and he split."

"What business?" Paul asked.

"Over on Thompson. Crosby Metalworks. I think he's like a welder or something." Anya shrugged.

We drank in silence for a moment and I thought about the wealth of intel I'd just gathered on Zane. I shouldn't care, I told myself. I didn't need to know much of anything beyond that he wasn't a serial killer and that he'd pay rent. But the idea of him as some kind of tortured loner pulled at me, twisting up an emotional response I definitely didn't need to explore.

"So..." I said, hoping to shift the conversation. "I need a date."

"Woot!" Anya hooted. "Yes you do! Bout time, girl."

I sighed. Anya had met her wife a few years ago and since then had been on a low-key mission to couple me up too. I had been largely resistant. "Not like a real date," I amended. "Just for this wedding at Christmas time."

"Why is she having a Christmas wedding again?" Paul asked.

I shrugged. "But she's been uber clear that if I don't find my own date, Rex's mother will assign me to his brother."

"Hot brother?" Anya asked. She knew Chelsea, but neither of us had met her soon-to-be brother-in-law. I'd been warned, though.

I shook my head. "Hot on the outside maybe. Not the kind of guy you want to be linked to once he opens his mouth. Arrogant, irritating... you get it."

Anya's nose wrinkled and she sighed the word, "Men."

"Hey!" Paul lifted his chin.

She shrugged again.

"Take hot roommate," Anya suggested. "Is he single?"

"No idea, but that would muddy the lines, don't you think?" I thought about it. I didn't think Zane would appreciate me assuming that just because we lived together he would be willing to save me from being set up with Chelsea's brother-in-law to be.

"I guess," Anya said. She angled her head at Paul. "Take him."

I looked at my friend and co-worker who resolutely shook his head.

"That would definitely muddy the lines," he said.

"It would just be a favor," I told him.

"It would be a problem," he said.

I began my second glass of beer while he explained.

"Men and women who are both over the median of attractiveness have a hard time with these types of romantic-tension-laced events when there's alcohol around. It's a well-studied phenomenon. We dress up, we drink, we witness the ultimate declaration of romantic love, and then go to a party designed to celebrate and promote that exact thing... and the potential for confusion mushrooms. And if we cross the line, we can't uncross it."

"We would not cross the line," I told him, but my heart wasn't in the argument. I didn't want to take Paul. I'd grown comfortable with the idea that I might not ever meet my person, but there was a part of me that still hoped. "I'll just find someone on the app. It'll be fine."

"The app." Anya frowned. "Because it's so reliable."

"You met Alex on the app!" I pointed out.

"The app under discussion is for straight people," she said. "And I met a woman on it. Do you see the inherent issue?"

I smiled at her. "Seems like it works great. And there's other apps."

"In this town, they'll have the exact same people on them. You need fresh meat," she said.

"You know, I might be convinced," Paul sighed, looking like

this conversation bored him. "We'll negotiate a raise in exchange."

"If only I could. You know I'd give you a raise." I shook my head.

"No. Don't take Paul. You should take a romantic potential," Anya said. "Alex knows some guys from work." Alex was a doctor in the next town over.

I sighed just as a text popped up on my phone screen.

**Chelsea: Got a date yet?**

The woman was telepathic. Crap. "Okay, Anya. I'm open to suggestions."

"I'll gather some applications from Alex's ideas." She smiled and bounced in her chair. "This will be fun."

I was pretty sure it would not be fun.

That night when I got home, the house was dark and quiet. I remedied that immediately by crashing into one of the little chairs at the table as I mis-negotiated the darkness in my slight inebriation. The chair went flying, hitting the end of the kitchen counter with a resounding clatter.

Seconds later, I heard a door open down the hall upstairs and a moment later, the living room was flooded with light.

I froze as my cheeks heated and turned to face my new roommate. "Sorry, I—" my explanation died on my lips as I took in the guy I'd invited to live in my house.

His hair was perfectly mussed on his head, and his dark soulful eyes were trained on me in a way that made me want to pull all my clothes off immediately.

Maybe that was the alcohol talking.

But the thing that really got my attention was the lack of a thing. Specifically, a shirt.

Zane came down the stairs, tattoos snaking across the most perfectly sculpted chest I'd ever seen in real life, his smoldering gaze doing things to my insides and stealing my breath.

"Are you okay?" he asked, his eyes sliding to the overturned chair.

"Yes," I said, pulling my own gaze back where it belonged. Which was anywhere but Zane's smooth golden skin, his deliciously muscled shoulders and arms, that tempting cord of muscle that formed a "v" and led right down into those low-slung pajama pants.

I moved to right the chair just as he did the same, and I found myself squatting low, his hand on mine along the back of the chair frame. Heat flung itself up my arm, and spread through my body.

"I got it," I said, clearing my throat and pulling myself back to a standing position, the chair between us.

"You sure you're okay?" Any irritation in Zane's voice was gone now, replaced with concern that sounded sincere. Somehow that was worse.

"I'm fine. Sorry for disturbing you. I had a few beers, and just kind of misjudged the, uh... the world." I risked a glance at him and a careful smile.

The look on his face was inscrutable. Was he annoyed? Or was there something else there in that dark hungry gaze?

"You didn't disturb me," he said. "I was just worried that you'd been hurt."

"I'm okay," I said again. "Just not too bright."

"Don't do that."

I frowned. "What?"

"I don't know you well, but I've spoken with you enough to know that you're wickedly intelligent. So don't discount that. Not even if you're kidding."

"Oh, um. Okay." A little flicker of pride lit inside me. Zane thought I was smart.

Shit. I *was* smart. I didn't need him to tell me that. What was happening here? All the intimations Anya had made about how I should ask Zane to the wedding were messing with my head.

Zane moved past me to the kitchen and poured a glass of water from the pitcher in the refrigerator. He handed it to me. "Need some ibuprofen?"

I shook my head. Why was he being so nice? "Thanks."

Those dark eyes found mine again and softened as he held my gaze a beat longer than was comfortable. "You're welcome."

"How's your dad?" I asked him. He'd mentioned that he was only in town to help his dad recover from something, but I wasn't sure what the situation was.

"He's..." Zane paused and trouble flitted through those incredible eyes. "He's getting better," he said finally. "Thanks."

I nodded, at a loss for how to navigate the raging attraction I was feeling for the shirtless man in front of me.

This whole roommate thing was going to be much harder than I'd thought.

"Well, goodnight," I told him.

"Goodnight Sabrina."

# Chapter Six

## Zane

I spent most of that first week visiting Dad in the hospital and then going over to the shop. Dad had given me the key after delivering a stern warning about not touching anything. For the first two days, I didn't. The place was a wreck. Half the lights were burned out and the floor was covered in dust and debris.

The apartment upstairs was worse.

I put it all back together slowly, alternating chores there with calls back to Johnathan at my own shop. I still didn't have much of a plan, because it wasn't quite clear to me what the next step was with Dad.

The world was a weird place. I went to bed that first five or six nights in a row telling myself it was a good thing Dad was sick because if he wasn't, I'd have too much mental energy on my hands. And time. And all that energy and time would inevitably begin to focus themselves in one place.

On one person.

Sabrina.

I didn't know my roommate well, but I had come to understand her a bit through a series of little actions she probably didn't even realize she did.

She scattered the seeds from her cantaloupe atop an old stump in the back yard, and a family of squirrels came out every morning to feast while I drank coffee at the kitchen window.

She set the coffeemaker for me so all I had to do was push a button and my cup made itself.

She left notes for me around the house:

*I left you a teeny bit of half and half. I'll pick up more today.*

*There's a croissant in the box that won't last another day. You should eat it.*

*I'll be home late. Will try not to drunkenly rearrange furniture and wake you again.*

They were small things. Roommate things, I guessed. But they were thoughtful things. And added all together, these tiny things took time, and that showed me that Sabrina was the kind of person who gave to others, who wanted things to be good and right, and who didn't always put herself first.

I tried to reciprocate.

I brought half and half home from visiting Dad and texted her not to worry about it. I ate the croissant, but replaced it with a box of strawberry-iced PopTarts, which she'd mentioned were her favorite. I waited up.

Friday night, two weeks after moving into Sabrina's house, I rode home from the hospital with uncertainty at war with fear inside me. Dad was going to be released the next day.

The doctor had brought me multiple brochures for assisted living facilities, but Dad refused to even look at them, and his anger over the entire topic made me think maybe he really didn't need them. He was the same grumpy guy, just a little sick. He needed time to recover—that was all.

"So you want to go home?" I asked him.

"Where the hell else would I go, Zane?"

"The doctor thinks maybe it's time to sell the shop? Move to a place where you have more help?"

Dad's glare told me what he thought of that idea.

Right. "Should I maybe stay with you? To help out?"

"Goddammit, Zane, this whole Florence Nightingale thing is driving me nuts."

I looked up Florence Nightingale before deciding whether to be annoyed at this comment.

"So no, then?" I swallowed, not meeting his eyes. We didn't tend to look each other in the eye when we spoke. That was the result of too many years of purposely trying to make the other angry, I guessed.

"No. I want to go home. Alone." He didn't say anything else, and he turned away from me in the bed, cranking up the volume on SportsCenter. Now that he was feeling stronger, any gratitude for my presence had evaporated. The stern, silent wall of Dad was back.

I tried to imagine the two of us in his little apartment. The place where I'd grown up. It wasn't hard to imagine because I'd lived there until I'd turned seventeen. When Dad had kicked me out. No. I couldn't live there.

But Dad needed help.

The doctor had provided the number for a partially state-funded recovery aide that Dad's insurance would help pay for, so I'd called and set everything up.

And as I sat on the couch at Sabrina's, nursing the second beer of the evening, I ignored the dread bubbling inside me at what the next few weeks might hold. Dad was not the guy I remembered. But he was the same man who'd sent me away at seventeen with nowhere to go, no plans for my life, and only a high school diploma to my name.

In a decade, I'd changed all of that. And I'd even thought about trying to rebuild the relationship with my father—mostly for Mom's sake. But the scars were there, and sometimes they ached.

I was lost in thought when the front door clicked open, and Sabrina stepped in, the cooling fall air rushing in around her, along with a few crackling leaves.

"It's windy out there!" Her cheeks were flushed, and her eyes sparked, taking in everything about the room and meeting mine briefly before dancing away. She closed the door behind her and moved to drop her enormous bag onto the table. "How're you?"

Sometimes I spent so much time in silence I wondered if my voice even worked. I tried it out. "Yeah. Okay. Good."

She turned back to me and lifted a brow. "When people say 'yeah, okay, good,' I think it means 'not so good.'" She went to refrigerator and pulled out a beer for herself, lifting it in a silent question. I gave her a quick nod and she brought me another.

"You have big plans tonight, Zane?" she asked as she held the beer out to me, taking the chair at the end of the coffee table.

The energy in the room had changed palpably since she'd entered, and the darkness inside me receded slightly. "This is pretty much it," I told her, trying for a smile.

"Everything okay with your dad?" She took a long drink from the bottle, and I found myself staring hungrily at the column of her pretty throat. Smooth, pale, and long. I imagined sliding my palm up that smooth skin, and did my best to cut the thoughts off right there.

"Yeah. He gets released tomorrow. Then some recovery at home, some physical therapy and stuff."

She nodded. "That's great. So he's going to be okay."

"As much as he can be okay, I guess."

The beer bottle paused halfway to her mouth. "I sense some less-than-good vibes between you and your dad."

"Perceptive."

"I'm sorry. That's hard."

People apologized all the time, but for some reason, I felt like she meant it. "Yeah. It is."

"So if you grew up here, do you have friends you used to hang out with? Anyone still around?"

I shook my head. "I wasn't really the friendly type back when I was in school. I guess I had friends in elementary school..." I trailed off.

She waited, and for whatever reason—maybe the third beer hitting my bloodstream—I decided to talk as she crossed her legs and waited.

"I wasn't super invested in school," I started. "I mean, I did well when I was little. But my mom died when I was in sixth grade, and after that...I guess I was angry."

I glanced at Sabrina, and found her bright eyes watching me intently, her lips in a soft little 'o'. "That's so hard," she whispered.

"Dad became a different guy. And as I got older and started working at the shop, I was basically his emotional punching bag."

"Oh Zane. Did he ever—"

"No. He never touched me. But he was grieving, and he didn't know how to handle it. So he took it out on me." I raised my beer. "Ten years of therapy."

"So good that you understand it, though," she said, raising her beer in return. "I'm sorry. That had to be a really tough way to grow up."

"It was." I could acknowledge it now. "I left when I was seventeen. Neither of us could stand the sight of the other without Mom around, and once I'd fixed up my first bike and assured myself it could get me at least a few states west, I took off." I swallowed hard, the truth rising up in me. "He kicked me out, actually."

"So young," she said on a breath. "What did you do?"

"I could weld, thanks to Dad," I said, staring at a ring of liquid on the glass tabletop and then wiping at it with my palm. "So I worked when I got to Denver. Met up with my cousin, who was older. He'd been good to me when I was young. He let me crash with him, and I got my own place. Eventually, my own shop."

"What kind of shop?" She sat up a bit.

"Metalworks," I said. "It was all I knew how to do."

"So what kinds of things do you make there?" Her bright eyes danced when she asked this, like she was really interested in hearing about welding.

"I started with repairs. Welding things back together, or fabricating easy things like simple fences. Whatever people needed. But I started playing with shapes and different kinds of metal, and eventually I started creating more artistic forms. Even sculpt a bit."

"You're an artist," she said, with clear appreciation in her voice.

I was. That was a title I'd recently accepted. And I was proud of that. "Yeah."

"Do you have anything I could see?" Sabrina bounced out of her seat, and before I even really thought about what was happening, she planted herself close at my side, our shoulders practically touching. She nodded to my phone on the table, expectant.

"Um. Yeah."

I swiped through my phone ad showed her a few of the sculptures I was most proud of—women in athletic poses—dancers, yogis, swimmers.

"These are incredible," she said. She turned and caught my

eye as a blush rose in her cheeks. "They're pretty sexy," she added.

"I didn't mean for them to be that," I told her, though I could acknowledge that they were—how could they not be when the subject matter itself was inherently beautiful? "I'm just drawn to the form."

"The female form," she clarified.

"Ah, yeah." Suddenly, things felt awkward. I slugged the rest of my beer just as Sabrina's phone pinged from across the room and she rose to pick it up. To my surprise, she returned with it to the spot next to me on the couch.

She sighed loudly as she looked at whatever had popped up on her phone.

"Good news, then," I said, trying to lighten the mood, and working to stifle the draw my roommate had over me. I wanted to lean in, to make her look at me again with those startling green eyes. I wanted to touch her, to kiss her.

I turned a bit to face her more, effectively putting more space between us.

"I guess," she said, a tiny mirthless laugh escaping her. She glanced up at me and then down again quickly. "I'll just tell you." She'd made a quick decision about something, and a second later I understood that she was embarrassed. "My friend Anya is basically sending me applicants for dates. Like my own personal dating app."

"You should try putting up a flier, maybe. Works for roommates."

She laughed, meeting my eyes again, and I my mood lifted, my blood heating and my body tightening immediately.

"I need a date to my friend's wedding."

"When is it?" I asked.

"December."

"You've got time."

"Historically, I'm pretty picky. It might take that long."

I watched her scroll on her phone.

"Want some help?"

"You want to help me pick dates?"

I hated the idea suddenly, but I'd already offered. "Sure. Another set of eyes."

And just like that, I'd become accomplice to Sabrina's efforts to choose some other guy who might have the opportunity to touch that soft smooth skin, to hear her laugh.

I was the biggest idiot on earth.

# Chapter Seven

## Sabrina

On Saturdays, I opened the shop a little later than during the week, since we didn't have the early morning off-to-work crowd to serve. I spent the morning at home, drinking coffee, chatting with my mom on the phone, making breakfast, and doing the weekly crossword on my tablet. Or at least that was what I did on Saturdays before Zane moved in. When I'd lived with Chelsea, she usually spent the weekends with Rex, so I often had the place to myself.

But this Saturday, I was met in the kitchen by a sleepy, shirtless Zane, and I had to put my responses to all that skin in check as I handed him a cup of coffee.

"Sleep okay?" I asked, trying not to think too much about him in the bed just beyond the wall of my own bedroom, all those muscles at rest in the sheets, all that sex appeal just waiting there...

He made a sleepy noise—like a half grunt—before meeting my eyes with a smile that was so bare and unguarded I wondered if I'd just gotten my first glimpse of the real Zane. Once he'd had a few sips of coffee, the shutters clicked back over his eyes and the smile dimmed, became practiced.

"Sleep is one thing I never have trouble with," he said, lifting the cup toward me in a little salute.

"Well, that's lucky." I thought about all the nights I'd wandered the house in the wee hours, wishing for sleep but finding only anxiety. "I'm jealous."

"You don't sleep?"

"I mean... I do. Just, sometimes my brain takes over."

He nodded. "I get that."

I moved back to the table with my coffee, partially to return to my eggs before they cooled, and partially to put some distance between myself and all the skin on display in the kitchen.

"So your dad gets out today?"

"Yep." Zane was quiet, and didn't add anything else, so I thought it best not to push on that topic too much.

"And are you going to work at the shop again today?" I asked. He said he'd been in his dad's metalworks shop, completing the orders he found and making sure things didn't get too far behind.

He sighed and sat across from me. "I might. There's not a lot else I can do without Dad to tell me what's supposed to be what. His organizational system is not great." Zane rubbed a hand through his spiky hair, and a pang of wild jealousy shot through me. I wanted to touch it. It was irrational, but it looked so soft and thick. "I just don't want him to get into trouble—he needs to be able to pay the mortgage on the building. It's not just his business, it's his home."

I nodded. Zane had told me before that he grew up living in the apartment over the metalworks shop, which I'd never really noticed before.

"He's lucky he has you to help him," I said.

Zane just nodded without meeting my eyes, and I assumed the topic was closed. The way he moved around the kitchen keeping his actions small and somehow focused anywhere but on me made me wonder if we were done speaking altogether, but then he came to the table, his coffee and a piece of toast in his hands. "Let's see some candidates," he said, taking the seat at my side and gesturing toward my phone.

"What?" My mind raced. What was he talking about?

"The guys your friend sent. Let's see it."

"Oh. Now?"

"Definitely. Who've we got?"

Zane wanting to help me sort through the abundance of random dudes Anya had sent still felt strange. Nonetheless, I pulled my phone toward me, laying it face up between us on the table.

I pulled up the first text she'd sent, steeled myself and scrolled down to the photo and description. "Umm... Phil?"

Zane frowned down at my phone. "We'll call him Phil McCracken."

I frowned and raised my eyes to Zane. "What?"

"Fill my crack in."

I couldn't contain the laughter that shot out of me. It was so out of character for Zane—so goofy. "Well, now he's off the table. I wouldn't be able to sit across from him and not think about you saying that."

A flicker of a smile crossed Zane's perfect lips and then he took a bite of toast, speaking around it. "Who else?"

I swiped. "Caleb?" I glanced at him for a nickname.

"Got nothing," he said. "Tell me more about Caleb."

"He's an engineer. He enjoys poetry. He—"

"He's a liar. Next."

I sat up and turned to face Zane. "Why? Because he says he likes poetry?"

Zane nodded, his mouth full of toast again.

"Some men like poetry."

Zane finished chewing. "Some men do. He, however, does not."

"You don't know that."

"You can tell. He might as well be wearing a sign that says, 'I hate poetry but think ladies will find me deep if I say I like it.'"

I stared at Caleb's photo. He did not especially look like a guy who liked poetry, but I didn't make a habit of assuming I knew anything about people based on their looks. "I don't think you can judge people that way."

Zane shrugged.

"When I first saw you, do you think I would have believed you were an artist?"

"I'm a welder."

"The sculptures you showed me last night say otherwise."

"You think Caleb here writes poetry?" Zane pointed at the image on my phone.

"I have no idea. I'm just saying, I think you should take people at face value until they give you reasons to think differently. Give them the benefit of the doubt."

Zane squinted at me, and I had the sense he was digging deep into me, seeing something I wasn't necessarily ready to show him. "Your outside definitely doesn't represent your insides, does it?"

I straightened, held his gaze even though I felt called out. "What do you mean?"

"The hair, the dark eye makeup. The nose stud, the tattoos."

"You have tattoos!"

He nodded. "They were a rebellion of sorts."

"So are mine, I guess." I dropped my eyes to my arm, considering the swan that sat on my forearm, its graceful neck climbing the length of my arm. There were others, too, but Zane didn't know about those.

"You wear armor." He said it simply, and it was just as hard to deny as it was to accept that he saw more than I'd invited him to.

"Maybe." I swallowed hard. "It started as a way to stand out."

He raised an eyebrow and lifted his coffee to his lips, waiting.

"I have a huge family. Lots of siblings. And a twin."

"There's another Sabrina running around?"

I shook my head. "Definitely not. Peter—that's my twin—Is literally nothing like me. We're fraternal, obviously. So we don't even look alike."

"How many others?"

"There's me and Peter, we're the babies. Then Stella and Ruby, the oldest. Chris and Dominic are in the middle."

"That's a lot," Zane agreed.

"Especially when they're all brainiacs and sports stars. My life consisted of being dragged from one event to another, and my job was celebrating every single one of my siblings and all of their amazing accomplishments."

Zane said nothing, but those dark eyes remained on my face, interested. Invested, even.

"And I was just me."

"What about your twin? You close?"

I lifted a shoulder. Peter had always looked out for me. If anyone got how out of place I felt in my family, it was him. But he had no problem fitting in. He was just as extraordinary as every one of my siblings. "Yeah, we are."

Zane finished his toast and leaned back in his chair. After a moment he met my eyes. "So maybe you're right."

"Okay," I said, watching Zane curiously.

"We should take people at face value. I like that you trust people. I'm also glad no one has given you reasons to be suspicious of people."

"Thanks?" I thought about what he was saying and realized that Zane didn't trust people because no one had given him good reasons to trust them. On his own at seventeen and forced to figure everything out himself? It must have been hard. Of course he'd be careful. My own childhood looked pretty idyllic in comparison. "You probably think I'm naive."

He sat up, fixing me with those dark soulful eyes. "What? Why would you say that?"

"Just..." I decided to let it go. "Nothing. Never mind. So is Caleb here a yes? Even with the question about his poetic leanings?"

"Do you find him attractive?"

I considered Caleb's photo. His hair was light brown and cut close, and he had a scruff of facial hair over pale skin. His eyes looked friendly, like maybe he laughed a lot, and I had the feeling he was a nice guy. As I considered, my brain was doing mutinous things. Like comparing every aspect of the perfectly available and nice-looking guy in the photo with the edgy, shirt-less, ridiculously sexy man at my side. The man who was my roommate. The man who I definitely should not be comparing to anyone I might go on a date with.

I sighed. "I don't know."

Zane laughed. "You don't know?"

I dropped my head into my hands. "Why is this hard?"

"Okay, if you don't know if he's hot, then he's not. So that's a no to Caleb."

We scrolled through six more guys, Zane alternately giving them nicknames that would make them impossible to date no matter how close to ideal they might be, and me missing even the tiniest spark of attraction for the others. After about ten candidates had been vetoed, I was back to square one, and also curious why Alex had access to so many single men. Maybe I was living in the wrong town.

"This is probably not going to result in a date for Chelsea's wedding," I told him. "You're too picky."

"You told me you were picky. I'm just helping. You can't date someone named Russell unless you're willing to have him be called 'Russell the love muscle.' This is common sense."

I burst into laughter, letting some of the tension release. "That's not common sense. That's insane. But now I'll never be able to date anyone named Russell!"

"For the best," Zane said, pushing his chair back and standing.

"You're impossible," I laughed, loving the easy banter I felt developing between us and then quickly tamping down the feeling.

Nothing to see here. This was not a thing.

Zane put his cup and plate into the dishwasher. "I better head over to the hospital."

"Good luck today."

He didn't respond, turning from the sink with a resolute acceptance on his handsome face.

I cleaned up my own dishes, listening to the sound of the shower upstairs and trying desperately not to think about the other half of Zane unclothed. I was nursing a growing fantasy about my hot roommate, and it was going to become a problem.

That night after work, I went to Anya's house for a glass of wine. Her toddler had just been put down to bed and Anya and Alex sat close together on the couch facing me.

I'd nursed my wine while they'd tag-teamed Charlie's bedtime routine, all in a well-coordinated dance between them.

"Impressive parenting," I told them when they both held a glass in their hands.

"More like well-executed crisis management," Alex laughed. "That's what parenting feels like at this age, anyway. I don't know when the real stuff starts."

"This is the real stuff," Anya laughed. "The fears and hopes and dreams, the stuffed animals and big hugs. This is what parenting is."

Alex looked at her skeptically. "Is it? Or is it breaking curfew and learning to drive, and first kisses and failing chemistry?"

"Eek." Anya took a big swig of her wine. "I think parenting is worrying. No matter the ages, there's always so much shit to worry about."

"That," Alex said, touching her glass to Anya's. "That's why there are two of us."

I loved watching them. And I hated it. I so enormously wanted something like they had—the easy companionship, the complete trust and adoration, the knowledge that someone had their back all the time. In everything.

"Why do you look like that?" Anya asked me, as if she'd just realized I was still sitting there.

"Like what?"

"You look disappointed with us," Alex supplied.

I shook my head quickly. "No! Not at all, not with you. I'm so impressed by you guys. And honestly? I'm really jealous."

"You want to spray the monster spray next time you're here? I'll let you," Alex said.

"I do," I said honestly. "I want all of it."

They both listened, not speaking, so I went on.

"I want what you have. The love. The friendship. The knowledge that for somebody out there, you're it. You're everything."

"You are everything," Anya said, and I hated the note of pity I heard in her voice.

I sighed and sipped my wine. "I could be," I said. "But I can't seem to find the person who realizes it."

"We realize it," Alex said. "But I do understand what you mean. We have each other. And even if we love you, we're not your person."

I pointed a finger at her. "That. Yes. You're each other's people." I shook my head. "I just... I looked through all those guys you sent today," I told Alex. "And I realized I don't even know if I know what I want? Like, what am I even looking for in life? Is it that? A date?"

Alex and Anya exchanged a look.

"Bigger than a date for sure," Anya said.

"Let's figure it out," Alex said, putting on her analytical voice. "So if you had to pick the thing you really want in the next year, what is it?"

Now I felt kind of silly. Like a little girl in a princess dress dreaming about her perfect wedding. "I just want someone to love, I guess," I said.

Anya nodded. "Well, I'm kinda thinking that you might have to cut your hours a little bit to give yourself time to find someone. As it is, if Prince Charming doesn't walk directly into Brewed Awakening, you'll never find him."

"You do work a lot," Alex said.

"It's my shop. I have to. And if I'm going to open a second location, I'll be working even more."

"Do you have to?" Anya asked.

"Do I have to what?"

"Work all the shifts? How's the business? Could you hire someone else? Like a manager or something?" she asked.

I considered. I could. The business was great, actually. "I mean, it's not like I have anything else to do."

"But you'd like to have something else to do," Anya pointed out.

"Or some ONE," Alex said, winking dramatically.

"And you can't have a life if you're working all the time."

I thought about that. I did work seven days a week, most of the hours the shop was open. And it had made it almost impossible to move forward with plans for a second shop in the next town over where a lot of commuter traffic made a coffee shop a dire need. "You might be right."

A manager, though? Given how hard it was to find a roommate, it might be tough to find a manager. Although, when it came to business, things seemed a lot easier than they did in my personal life.

"I'm always right," Alex said.

"Don't be smug," Anya told her.

"You like it when I'm smug," Alex shot back.

And they were off again, doing that couple thing where they spoke their own language and made it clear that for them, there was no one else in the world.

We talked about other things for the rest of the night, but my mind had stepped through the door they'd opened, and I found myself thinking hard about the life I'd built and the box I'd created for myself. Maybe it was time to open it up just a bit.

# Chapter Eight

## Zane

Dad was happy to be released from the hospital, but his good mood lasted about five minutes once I got him back home.

"What happened up here?" he asked, looking around.

What had happened was that I'd finally broken down and had the place cleaned. Professionally. I'd considered doing it myself, but in the fifteen years since I'd set foot in this two-bedroom apartment, either it had grown in general griminess and disrepair, or my standards had risen substantially. I wondered if Dad had ever cleaned, actually.

Now, the kitchen gleamed—as much as that was possible for a kitchen layered in tired linoleum and stocked with ancient appliances. At least the toilet had been returned to a semi-white state and the floors weren't sticky. Dad's stacks of magazines and newspapers had been culled to a less oppressive size, and the place didn't smell like dead things.

"I had it cleaned."

That earned me a glare.

I'd just gotten Dad settled in his recliner when the doorbell rang.

"Who the hell is that?" Dad seemed to have forgotten everything we'd discussed on the way home. The conditions of his release to his own house.

"That'll be the aide," I reminded him.

"Tell him to get lost."

I sighed, pulling open the door and reminding myself once again that this was temporary, that soon I'd be back in Denver, and Dad could go on being angry and impossible and it wouldn't affect me. Only, something inside me had changed. I wasn't sure what, but I wanted something I didn't think I'd wanted before. The last time I'd been in Holly Creek, I'd wanted only to escape. Now? I wasn't sure. But the devil on my heels had slowed his pace.

"Hi there," I said to the smiling woman on the doorstep wearing scrubs.

"Hi," she said, sticking out a hand for me to shake. "You must be Zane. I'm Valerie. From CareLight."

"Valerie," I repeated, shaking her hand gently. "Well, I'm glad you're here, but Dad might take a bit more to win over."

She laughed lightly and hoisted her bag higher on her shoulder. "Trust me, I've seen it before."

"Come on in." Valerie followed me in, dropping her bag to the floor inside the door, and we approached Dad, who hadn't forgotten how to use the television remote—or the volume button, apparently.

"Dad," I practically shouted over the baseball game he'd found. "This is Valerie. She's here to help you."

"Don't need help," Dad said, not even looking up.

I snapped. Dad could be rude to me, but he was the one who had taught me to be polite to other people. He was behaving like a toddler, and I'd had enough.

Valerie began to say hello, but I put up a hand for her to wait, while I picked up the remote and pressed mute.

"What the hell—"

"Let's try again," I suggested, meeting my father's angry glare. "Dad, this is Valerie. She's here to help you."

He sneered at me, but then sighed and turned to Valerie. "Don't need help," he said, but his words lacked the energy he'd put into his glare.

"That's okay, Mr. Crosby, I'll find plenty to do until you do need help. Why don't I start by making us some lunch?" she asked cheerfully.

Dad shrugged and gave up, reclining the chair and closing his eyes. He'd evidently sapped all the energy he had for the day.

"I'm sorry," I told Valerie. "He's used to doing everything himself. I think this heart attack really scared him. I don't think change is going to be easy for him."

"Change is tough for everyone," she said, heading for the kitchen. "Do you live here too, Zane?"

I followed her, impressed by the easy authority she possessed as she began pulling things from the refrigerator I'd just restocked. Soon, she was at the counter making sandwiches as if she'd lived here for years.

"No," I said, taking a seat at the table. "I'm just in town to get Dad settled again. I live in Colorado."

"Ah," she said, nodding. "Well, it'll just take me a day or two to figure things out here, and then I expect you'll be on your way whenever you're ready to end your visit."

"A day or two," I repeated, surprised.

"Yep. I'll share duties with three other aides, one of whom will be here overnight just in case Ben needs anything. The rest of us work eight-hour shifts, and we're here for just about anything besides medication. We can remind him what to take when, we just aren't allowed to give it to him."

They'd explained all that on the phone when I'd booked the service. "Great. Okay." I thought about the other things they'd explained on the phone. Like the overwhelming cost of full-time care. For now, I had some savings that would cover it, and the state and insurance helped for a limited time. Hopefully Dad would spring back. But if not, I'd need to make some decisions.

I stayed with Dad and Valerie for a few hours, pleased to see that Dad mellowed a bit as he grew used to her presence. Her bright blue eyes and overall appearance didn't hurt either. Little did CareLight know, Dad had a thing for redheads with generous curves, and after a little while, he was flirting shamelessly with Valerie in a way that she clearly was used to.

"You'll call me if there are any problems?" I asked as I left.

"That's why we're here," she assured me.

"I'll be downstairs in the shop for a bit, and then I'm just a few blocks away."

"Do what you need to do. I've got it handled. And Sophie will be here later."

I nodded, and said goodbye to Dad, who seemed to have shifted into a much more pleasant mindset, where maybe he thought Valerie was here for a date. Poor Valerie.

As I was parking my bike at the curb in front of Sabrina's place, I noticed a car pulling up behind me. I took my time getting organized, and watched as a guy I remembered vaguely from high school stepped out of his shiny mini-SUV, smoothed his hair, and walked up the front pathway.

My brain spun, trying to remember the guy. Todd? Tad? Something like that. He'd been a douche in high school, and from what I could tell, not much had changed. More confusing was why he was standing on the front step of our place, looking nervous.

As the front door swung open, understanding dawned.

He was here for a date.

With Sabrina.

My stomach roiled and my blood heated before I had a moment to think rationally about this fact.

I followed him up the path and approached where Todd-Tad stood, Sabrina smiling just inside the door. She looked beautiful, her hair tousled to frame her face and those green eyes gleaming as she said hello to the guy in front of me. Then those incredible eyes slid to me, and her smile faltered slightly.

"Excuse me," I said, sliding past the guy. I moved inside, intending to ignore the whole situation. Who Sabrina dated was not my business.

"Roommate," Sabrina explained.

"I'm a few minutes early," Todd-Tad was saying. "But, ah..." he paused his train of thought in a way that didn't sound altogether good, and I hesitated just around the corner where Sabrina couldn't see me.

"Tattoos, huh?" he asked now.

Douchebag.

"Yeah," Sabrina said, her voice sounding softer than I was used to.

"Fun hair color there, too." Todd-Tad did not sound like he thought Sabrina's hair was fun and I had an unnerving urge to fly back to the door and punch him.

"Um," Sabrina had clearly picked up on his douchiness and I hated the uncertainty I heard in her voice.

I stepped back around the corner.

The guy on the doorstep pulled out his phone, and put on a show of checking it as if he'd just received a text. "Oh gosh," he said. "Listen, I might need a raincheck."

"Oh, ah. Okay," Sabrina said. She sounded defeated. I hated it.

"Yeah, shoot. I think I have to run. But I'll totally call you."

"Hey," I said, pulling the guy's attention to where I stood at Sabrina's side. "Didn't you graduate from Holly Creek High?"

"Uh, yeah. You are...?"

"Zane. Crosby." I chuckled. I was going to enjoy this. I went on, casually. "I feel like I remember you shitting yourself in biology class once... was that you?"

Todd-Tad's face dropped the smug expression. "What? No, I mean..." he cast a glance at Sabrina, paling. "I was really sick. I think the whole family had food poisoning," he said.

"Oh, right," I said conversationally. "Good that you can laugh about it now."

He frowned, clearly not quite to the stage where he could laugh about it.

"You're feeling okay tonight, though?" I asked. Sabrina elbowed me hard in the ribs.

"Uh, yeah, look. I really have to go." Todd-Tad scooted right off the porch, faster than he'd fled from biology all those years ago.

Sabrina closed the door, crossed her arms and turned to glare at me. "That wasn't very nice."

I ambled into the living room and then crossed to the kitchen to get a beer. "Him? Or me?"

"Either one of you, actually. But... maybe I owe you a thank you."

I handed her a beer after opening it for her, and then nodded. "I saved you. That guy is a tool. You don't want to date him."

"You're probably right, but Zane, you don't decide who I want to date!"

"You asked for my help."

"And you were not helpful. I figured we were done with that. I took matters into my own hands and asked Anya not to send me options, but to just set me up."

I frowned at her. "No offense, but Anya has horrible taste."

She glared at me for a second longer, but then the fire in her eyes simmered down to a glow. "Yeah, maybe. She's not really into guys, so..."

"Maybe not the best judge."

Sabrina sat on the couch and then pointed at me. "It's not like you're into guys either, though. Are you? How can you be a good judge?"

"Guys know guys," I said, the extent of my interference in my roommate's life beginning to sink in. "Still," I said. "I probably shouldn't have done that. I'm sorry."

She sniffed. "I don't think I wanted to go out with him anyway. Maybe you did save me."

I nodded.

"How's your dad?"

And just like that, Sabrina and I settled in and talked about our days for the next couple hours, finishing off the beer in the fridge and eventually ordering Thai food.

The late night found us curled into opposite ends of the couch, still talking.

"That's really expensive," Sabrina said after I'd admitted what full-time care for Dad was costing.

"The alternative was to sell his place and move him into a facility. I'll need to figure something out. I guess the dementia is only going to get worse. But there's still the chance he's not so bad off, and once he recovers from the heart attack, he might be fine for a few more years."

"Maybe." She didn't look like she had much faith in that outcome—and she hadn't even met Dad. "That's all so hard. Good thing you're a wealthy artist." I could tell by the way she said this that she knew it wasn't true.

"I've got some money saved, and some of the sculpture has sold pretty well, yeah. But I can't sustain this for more than a couple months without going into debt. Unless I sell the shop and the house in Denver."

"You own both of those? That's great."

I explained how I'd gotten lucky, buying city property before housing prices really skyrocketed. "And the shop was in foreclosure in a part of town most people didn't want to be in. But it was perfect for metalworking."

"Are you renting your place out while you're here?"

I stretched. "Yeah. Rebecca knew someone who needed a place, so she's there now."

"That's good."

"Yeah. She basically covers the mortgage."

"So you can just stay as long as you need to?"

"It's definitely not what I planned." I had commissions back in Denver that needed attention, but the guy I worked with, Johnathan, was handling those. So there was nothing pulling me back immediately, but my life was there.

Sabrina had stretched her legs out so that her feet pressed into my thigh, and there was something both electrifying and immensely comfortable in the contact. I tried to focus on the latter so I didn't end up thinking too much about the former.

"Got any more dates planned?" I asked her.

She stuck out her tongue at me. "I do, actually."

"Want me to vet this one in advance? I went to high school here. I know everyone in town."

She squinted at me and frowned. "Great."

"Who is it?"

She sighed. "Damian Frost?"

Oh shit. "You cannot go out with Damian Frost."

Sabrina let out a huff and pulled her feet back, putting them on the floor and standing. "And we're done here."

"Don't you even want to know why?"

"Did he have an embarrassing bathroom incident I need to be made aware of?"

I shook my head. "Worse."

She picked up our empty beer bottles and took them to the kitchen while I warred with myself about whether it was okay to poison her against guys who I had known more than a decade ago. Maybe they'd changed. But with Damian, I doubted it.

Finally, she came back to stand in front of me, looking painfully sexy in a fitted black tank and tight black jeans. The swan on her forearm danced as she put her hands on her hips. "I do not want to know," she said. "And your help with my dating life is definitely no longer needed."

"Definitely?"

"Definitely. But thanks."

"Oh." I watched Sabrina head upstairs to the bathroom and sat on the couch a few more minutes, until I'd heard her close herself in her room. I had a problem I didn't know how to fix. I did not want Sabrina going out with anyone but me. And I couldn't date her myself, since I didn't plan to stay in town more than another few weeks.

For a moment I toyed with the idea of seeing if she might be open to something more... casual, but I quickly pushed the idea away. She deserved more than that. I just wasn't the guy who could give it to her.

# Chapter Nine

## Sabrina

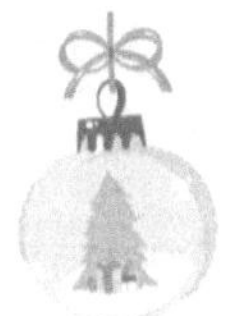

"Wait, Sabs. Who is Trent?" Paul frowned at the schedule.

"He's our new manager." I continued cleaning the expensive coffee machine I'd been working on all morning. When I was nervous, I power cleaned. And I was nervous about relinquishing my shop to Trent, despite the endorsements he'd received from Alex and Anya. Of course, they'd also set me up with the crappy date too, but I was willing to give them another shot.

"Manager?" Paul was standing a little too close, staring at me like a puppy demanding attention.

I sighed. "Yes. Manager. Remember when I asked you if you wanted to take on more hours and responsibility here?"

"Yes."

"And you said no."

"Also yes."

"So that meant I needed to find someone else to take on more hours and responsibility here. And that's Trent."

Paul frowned at me. "Oh."

"Yes. Oh."

"Why again? You know I fear change." Paul frowned at me, and I glanced at the clock. We were opening in ten minutes, and Trent should be here any second.

"Because change is good. And I want to open the second location, but I'm here so much I don't have time."

Paul nodded.

"Okay?" I asked him.

"Yeah. Okay."

"So be nice."

"Nice."

Just then, Trent appeared outside the glass door, and I went to let him in. I'd met Trent twice now, once on the phone right after my conversation with Alex and Anya about freeing up more time, and once a few days earlier when he'd come to see the shop and discuss the particulars of what I was looking for. He was older, and retired, but had managed several restaurants and specialty retail shops through his career and was looking for part-time work to get him out of the house.

"Hi Trent," I said, pushing the door open to allow him in.

"Good morning, Sabrina." He gave me a warm smile and looked around the space again appreciatively. "I'm very excited to be here this morning."

"I'm glad," I told him.

"The wife is also excited. She says having me home all day is cramping her style."

I laughed at that. "Well this is good for everyone, then. Come meet Paul. He's a veteran employee and will help with anything you need while you get up to speed." I directed this last part at Paul, who did not look quite as swarm and welcoming as I'd hoped he would after our chat.

"Hi." Paul delivered one word and then busied himself under the counter with something.

"He warms up," I promised Trent.

Soon, we were opening the door for the day and welcoming

guests, and Trent didn't hesitate. He told me the best way to begin was at the beginning, to learn the business as he would as an employee, so for now, Paul was bossing him around. But my hope was that Trent would be able to add some of his experience to mine and that he would be the magic key to unlock my ability to step away here and get the second location going. And maybe have a bit more free time eventually. To figure out what I really wanted out of my life.

After lunchtime, Trent was on break, and things were a little slow, so I took some paperwork to a table in the corner where the late fall sunlight was doing its best to wash the streets outside in yellow. The forecast called for snow. I was trying to soak up as much not-snow as I could while it lasted, when a familiar motorcycle pulled up to the curb and a tall, muscled rider gracefully swung himself off it, pulling the helmet from his handsome head and sending my blood suddenly hot through my veins. Zane.

The expression on his face as he approached wasn't happy, and I felt a bit like I was intruding, watching him when he wasn't aware I was watching. He strode toward the door and by the time he stepped inside, his face was set in the same stern expression he usually wore.

"Hey!" I called from where I sat.

He stopped and turned toward me, and the hard line of his lips eased into a smile as he came to take a chair at the table.

"Hi," he said, sitting. The tension in his body had eased visibly, and I got a warm little buzz, thinking it was due to me somehow.

"How are things?" I asked him.

He frowned. "Okay, I guess. Dad is warming up to his aides. He calls them his girls now and acts like I'm in the way when I'm there."

I smiled, but I could see that Zane didn't find it funny that his father continued to push him away. I couldn't even imagine what it would feel like to think my own family wouldn't welcome me warmly if I came home.

"The issue is more at the shop. He doesn't want me in there, but he's not capable of working right now. He can't move around heavy equipment and operate the machinery, and he won't let me help."

I shrugged. "Sounds like there isn't much you can do."

"I answer the phone when I'm in the shop, and he's got more than a few angry customers with late deliverables."

"You told them what happened to your dad though, right?"

"Of course. But there's money involved, and people expect him to finish the work."

"Yeah." That was hard.

"Tonight's the night, right?" Zane asked, tilting his head.

"The night?"

He wiggled his eyebrows.

"Oh, my date. With Damian. Yes."

"Where are you going?"

"The brewery on Main. Very public, very safe."

He made a grunting noise, and I waited for him to say more, but he kept his promise. It seemed that he was not planning to interfere. And after all, I didn't need to marry the guy. I just needed someone I could take to Chelsea's wedding. Someone who would be fun and personable, and having the guy be hot wouldn't be a bad thing either.

"Well, have fun," he said, looking like it practically pained him to say the words.

"I will."

"Gonna grab lunch and then head back to Dad's place."

I nodded, and tried to not stare as Zane went to the counter and picked out a sandwich, his jeans gripping his legs and butt as he bent over to pick it out of the refrigerated case. I also didn't stare at the way the tattooed muscles bulged from the arms of his black T-shirt as he pulled his wallet from his jeans to pay.

He gave me a sexy grin as he headed back out the door, and I continued not staring as he mounted his bike and revved off down the street, leaving me with an unwanted fantasy about my roommate. My very unavailable, very temporary roommate.

That night, I was sitting at the U-shaped bar inside Tap Meister waiting for Damian to show.

If nothing else, the guy had a pretty hot name. Damian Frost. Sounded like he'd be a character on one of those shows about vampires and teenagers.

When Damian arrived, his looks did not disappoint. He was blond, which was usually not my thing, but his hair was a dark blond, short, but longer on top, and he had a Chris Hemsworth kind of scruff going on that was very attractive. Anya had sent me a photo, so I was pretty sure this was him.

"Sabrina?" he said, approaching with a half-smile. He was tall, broad. So far, so good.

"Yes, hi. Damian?"

He winked in response.

One point off.

"Nice to meet you," he said, sliding onto the stool next to me. "You're hotter in person."

"Um. Thanks?"

"My photo does me justice, I know. I hired a pretty expensive photographer to do those headshots."

I nodded, uncertain what to say to his self-validating statement. "Well. Okay."

Another wink.

Oh no.

"You already on the sauce here?" he asked, pointing to the full glass of wine before me.

"Um. I just ordered," I said, my hopes sinking by the second.

Damian ordered himself a beer and a shot, and I tried to keep an open mind.

"Do you always order two drinks at one time?" I smiled and kept my tone light.

He frowned at me. "It's just a shot." The shot was disposed of quickly, and then my date leaned back, letting his gaze trail down my body, lingering on my legs, which suddenly felt inappropriately exposed in a very short leather skirt. "I like this whole edgy thing you've got going on. Very naughty."

I cleared my throat, determined to get the conversation going somewhere that didn't involve the way either of us looked. "So what do you do for work, Damian? Something in finance, you said?"

His mouth twisted up on one side into a wry smile, and he shook his head. "It's complex." The way he said this indicated clearly that he didn't think I'd be interested. Or maybe—god, I hoped not—that I wouldn't understand.

"Tell me about it," I suggested.

He frowned, and then sighed, as if giving in to a silly request. "Well, babe, I'm what you call a valuation analyst." He waited after uttering these words, as if I might already be confused.

"Right, so you determine the valuation of companies to help with investment or acquisition?"

Damian's eyebrows climbed. "Not just a pretty face, huh?"

I was about to respond when the door to the bar opened—which it had probably done at least ten times since I'd been sitting here, but this time some vibration in the atmosphere pulled my attention, a disturbance in the force, maybe.

Zane.

He shot me a cocky grin and then ambled around the bar to

the other side, seating himself directly across from where I sat with Damian.

Perfect.

Damian had decided I was worthy of a long diatribe about his job, and was droning on about reviewing debt and equity securities, valuation of IP, and all the different tools he needed to be an expert on to do this job.

But I could barely listen. When Zane was in a room, I couldn't help being focused on him. Even though I wasn't looking at him, and my body was angled toward Damian, Zane had my attention.

"I told you it was too complicated for you to understand," Damian concluded, taking my inattention for incomprehension.

"Sorry, no. I understand. I just got a little distracted for a second."

Damian looked around, his eyes landing on Zane.

"That loser's back."

I followed his gaze, certain he had to mean someone else. "Who?"

"That guy." He pointed baldly at Zane, drawing Zane's attention. "Went to high school with him. Total idiot. Looks like nothing's changed."

My blood was heating again, and indignation on Zane's behalf began threatening to make me say things I'd probably regret. "What do you mean?" I asked.

Damian returned his attention to me, and suddenly the hot body and perfect hair seemed almost repugnant. "He was all mopey and emo in school. Like he was putting on this loner persona he thought was hot or something."

"Maybe he was actually a loner."

"Maybe." Damian shrugged. "Going nowhere fast. Looks like he's arrived."

"He's an artist," I blurted, not intending to say anything else about my roommate.

Damian laughed. "You know that guy?"

"Yeah. I know him. And he's really talented. Smart." Damian's smile faded, and I couldn't help what came out of my mouth next. "Pretty hot, too."

"Hot?" Damian stood. "You like 'em dirty and dark, huh, babe?"

"I like them smart and self-possessed," I shot back, standing to face him. "And I like it when they don't call me 'babe.'"

Were we in a fight? This was getting awkward fast, and now Zane's attention was fully on the two of us, squaring up across the bar.

"Well, here's what I think," Damian said, his tone becoming immediately condescending. "I think you might be nice for a quick little roll in the car or maybe at a cheap hotel. But if you're looking for anything more than that, I'm pretty sure—"

"I'll just stop you right there," I said, taking a step back. "I'm not looking for anything. Especially not with you. This was a mistake."

Damian's mouth opened and then closed again, as he tried to wrap his head around the fact that he'd just been dismissed. I wondered for a second if anyone had turned the jerk down before. I couldn't imagine he got a lot of second dates with his "roll in the car" propositions.

He gave me a glare that lasted a beat too long as he digested the situation, then dropped a twenty-dollar bill on the bar and turned, leaving without another word. As soon as his big frame was out the door, I slumped back down onto my stool, suddenly exhausted and disheartened.

I was bad at dating.

I knew Zane was probably curious about whatever had just happened, but I couldn't bring myself to look at him. As much as I wanted to be mad at him for ruining yet another date, this one really wasn't his fault. And I was glad Damian had shown his true colors early instead of dragging me into something where they'd be revealed eventually, and I'd wind up hurt.

"Hey." Zane's low rumble came from over my shoulder. "You okay?"

Warmth spread through me at the comforting timbre I was coming to associate with good things—friendship, warmth, home.

I nodded miserably. "I think I'm done with dating."

"Nah," he said, a big hand landing on my shoulder and pulling my gaze to meet his, which was full of concern. "You'll find what you're looking for. You deserve to be happy."

I shook my head. "I'm happy on my own. I should quit trying to change that."

Zane seemed to think about that for a moment, then slid into the seat Damian had vacated. "I think people can definitely be happy on their own. But sometimes I wonder if sharing things—experiences and thoughts—can add another layer to what's already good."

I frowned at him. "Maybe. But if you think that, why are you still alone?"

His eyes closed for a long second, as if I'd wounded him, but when they opened, they were bright and clear.

"What if you try dating one more time?" he said. "Let me set you up."

I blew out a breath—half laugh, half frustration. "You're going to set me up?"

"I know a guy you might like."

On the heels of the raging success that was my date with Damian, I wasn't sure at all. But I did trust Zane.

"Fine. But this is the last one. After this, I'll just tell Chelsea I'm going stag to the wedding."

# Chapter Ten

## Sabrina

A week later, I pulled my coat tighter around me as I stood outside Chez Furet, a fancy French restaurant I'd only eaten at once. It wasn't in Holly Creek. It was actually in the next little town over, Garden Falls, where I was in the midst of negotiation for a storefront for my second coffee shop.

I'd just arrived, and was about to head inside to wait when the night filled with the rumble of a motorcycle pulling up to the curb across the street. I turned and watched in disbelief as Zane dismounted and stepped into the street, heading toward me with a smile on his face that looked somewhat uncertain. He'd managed to involve himself in both of my previous dates, and I'd made him promise not to show up and ruin this one.

He'd agreed, but now here he was.

"You promised," I reminded him when he arrived to stand next to me just outside the front door.

"I promised I wouldn't ruin this date for you."

"I know. And yet, here you are." I threw my hands up in the air. "What am I supposed to say when this guy shows up?"

"Hello?"

"Can you please go?"

"I could, but then you'd think your date stood you up."

I stared at him. "What?"

He didn't speak, just pulled open the door of Chez Furet and gestured for me to go inside. I did, but only because the wind was picking up and I was freezing out there on the sidewalk. I could be mad at Zane inside, where it was warm.

Zane followed me into the close space where the scent of bread and garlic was wafting around, making my mouth water.

"Bon soir," said the hostess behind the little table just inside the door. "Do you have a reservation?"

"Yes," Zane said. "Zane Crosby. For two."

I shook my head, anger bubbling hot in my veins. "You're eating here too? You knew this was where I was going. Why are you trying to ruin this?"

Zane looked down at me and smiled. "I am definitely not trying to ruin this."

"Right this way," the hostess said, waving us inside the intimate space.

Zane looked at me expectantly, and understanding began to dawn. I followed the hostess, Zane stepping close behind me and dropping a warm hand to my low back. Heat shot through me in anticipatory tingles, and I tried to will it away. I was angry, not turned on.

The hostess seated us in the back corner of the restaurant, situated us with menus, and then left us there together.

"You're my date?" I asked finally. "You tricked me."

Zane's dark eyes found mine and held them, a warm connection forming between us, which he finally broke with a heavy blink, dropping his eyes to the table. "I'm sorry," he said. "I didn't like seeing you with those jerks."

I swallowed, trying to process what was happening here. "Zane," I said slowly, waiting for that hot caramel gaze to meet mine again. "Did you bring me here because you didn't want me to go out with another jerk, or because you wanted me to go out with you?"

Zane held my gaze, and I could see clouds of emotion chasing each other through his eyes. Finally, he said, "Both. But mostly because I wanted you to go out with me, and I guess I wasn't sure you'd agree."

We sat with that admission for a while, and just as I was forming another question, the waiter arrived to talk about the menu and take our drink orders.

When we were alone again, I stared at the tablecloth, my fingers rearranging the forks lined up next to one another as I thought. Finally, I said, "I want to be angry at you for tricking me."

Zane didn't say anything, so I went on.

"But I'm finding it hard to be mad because I'm actually really happy to be on a date with you."

I heard him suck in a breath, as if I'd surprised him. "Really?"

"You had to know that," I said, finally risking a look up at him. "Or you wouldn't have done this."

He tilted his head slightly. "I hoped."

We'd just exchanged more honest conversation than I'd had in my last two dates combined, and the words worked to pull us tighter together, a delicate connection forged between us.

For the beginning of our time there in the dim French restaurant, with soft music lingering at the edges of the little bubble we'd formed, we were careful and quiet, talking with long pauses in the conversation as we each tried to test the thread connecting us without breaking it.

By the time a simple slice of apple tart sat on the table between us, two forks resting on the plate, that delicate connection had been reinforced through shared looks, laughter, conversation. And now it was a weighty rope, something we could rely on.

Zane's eyes held a familiarity and warmth that both reassured and excited me, and every time they met mine, heat flooded me, sending tingles of anticipation through my body.

"You've got just a bit here," he said, indicating a spot on his chin with his finger.

I wiped my chin with my napkin, but Zane chuckled and before I knew it, he was taking my jaw gently in his hand, using his own napkin to wipe a spot just below my lower lip. A shiver went through me at the touch.

Zane lowered his napkin, his eyes never leaving mine. His hand didn't release me. Instead, his thumb stroked a careful line across my lip, setting off another round of shivers through me, and I found myself leaning closer.

His eyes dropped to my mouth, and disparate words and disconnected thoughts flew through my mind. *Yes. Kiss. Want. Need.*

Zane moved closer still, until we were just centimeters apart, and then his eyes dropped shut and those firm sculpted lips met mine.

The kiss began tentatively, soft and seeking like a question, an uncertainty to be confirmed before we went any further. Without conscious thought, I found my hands reaching for him, finding his solid shoulder, the back of his neck, the soft strands of his hair. And as my hands searched, my lips opened and I pulled Zane in, closer, until our tongues met, asking and answering in a chaotic game of hide and seek that set my body on fire.

Zane's hand on my jaw tightened, angling my mouth for better access, and his other hand slid into my hair, cradling my head and pulling me toward him in one coordinated motion.

I might have given some thought to how we looked, making out in a fancy restaurant, but I was lost to the moment. I was sensation, music, the yeast-scented air swirling around us. I wasn't me in that moment—I was his. And yet, I was more me than I'd ever been.

Finally, we agreed by some unspoken understanding that it was enough, and our mouths reluctantly parted, but my forehead rested against his, his warm hand still on the back of my neck as we both breathed the other in. I regained myself and pulled back, feeling like I'd just popped my head through the surface of a deep lake. I was discombobulated, lost. But Zane was there, those dark eyes full of reassurance and desire, and all I wanted was to plunge into the murky depths again, to stay there this time.

"Should we go?" he asked me, his voice laced with danger and promise.

"Yes," I said, the apple tart between us forgotten.

Zane signaled for the check and then we were stepping back outside into the bracing cold, Zane's arm around my back, pulling me near as I handed him my car keys without even thinking about it.

"We can get your bike tomorrow," I suggested.

He made a low hum of agreement, and we slipped into my car, Zane driving us home while that connection between us seemed only to strengthen and grow over the course of the ride.

"Thank you," I said to him, barely loud enough to make myself heard over the hum of the engine. "I had a really nice time."

Zane met my gaze, and his eyes sparked. "I don't think I'm ready to say goodnight."

Relief swept through me. "Neither am I."

We parked in the darkness of the driveway next to the house and for a brief second, neither of us moved, as if we weren't sure quite how to proceed. Or because we were worried about shattering the atmosphere around us, the charged little bubble we found ourselves in together.

I let my fingers curl lightly around the door handle, and when I pulled, filling the truck cab with light as the door cracked open, the spell broke. Zane came around to my side, helping me out of the truck I got out of every single day just fine by myself. And I adored it.

He put his hand on the small of my back as we moved toward the back door, and kept it there while I unlocked the house and stepped inside. He closed and locked the kitchen door, and then we were there, in the space we shared, some new thing in the room with us that hadn't been there before.

Just as I was gathering myself to speak, Zane's fingers found my cheek, tracing a soft line along the side of my face. I heard myself sigh, and leaned into the touch, letting my own hands find the hard planes of his chest through the soft shirt he wore.

Zane pulled me closer, those deep dark eyes drilling into me, sending chain reactions of fireworks lighting through my veins.

"You're beautiful," he said, his voice a sandpaper whisper. And then his lips met mine again, and I felt the kitchen swirl away, the ground dropping from beneath my feet and mind filling with nothing but him. Zane. Tall and dark, and so achingly handsome.

Our mouths teased and tasted, a delicious push and pull of tongues, lips and breath. And we slowly inched back and upstairs to the bedroom Zane had occupied for the last few weeks. He pulled me inside, catching me in his arms and then pinning me against the wall just inside the door, where he dropped his head and set to work devouring my neck and drop-ping little kisses and nips all along my collarbone. In the moments when I was able to breathe, to think, I looked around the space I hadn't entered since he'd come to live here.

Nothing had changed. There was not a single sign that this room had an occupant, other than the boots set neatly next to the chair, and the jeans hanging in the open closet. There were no photographs, no hastily tossed T-shirts, nothing. I didn't know why exactly, but a deep sadness welled inside me at the realization, and I pulled Zane even closer, trying to—what?

Comfort him? I was the one who was sad at the clear impermanence of him here.

My fingers found the hem of his shirt and even as I imagined pulling it over his head, it was done, Zane helping me with a low rumbling grunt of desire that put every conscious thought from my mind. His golden skin spread before me, decorated with the scrolling filigree of tattoos tracing along his shoulder, down his arms. An orchid here, a complicated bird there.

I explored the fascinating landscape of him while he pulled me toward the bed, peeling my own clothes from my body as we went, and soon, we were wrapped up together beneath the fluffy duvet I'd bought when Chelsea left. We were arms and legs, bodies and breath, and I fought to keep my thoughts from interfering. Because I wanted Zane. Wanted him like this—commanding and dominating and so, so masculine. I didn't want to feel sorry for him, or worried for him. And didn't want to think about what would happen to my heart if I let myself think too much about the man in my arms beyond his physical presence right here, right now.

"I want to taste you," he whispered, his mouth worshipping my breasts as his hands touched and teased the rest of my torso. The weight of him was hot across my hips, and now he slid lower, leaving me feeling exposed and chilly until—

"Oh god," I said, feeling the flat of his tongue swiping up over my most sensitive skin, once, twice more, and then delving into my folds and finding the spot that had me gasping.

Zane's hands and mouth worked in concert, and whatever thoughts I'd been struggling to release flew from my mind as he coaxed me closer and closer to release. I could feel my legs shaking, my entire body shuddering, and I heard sounds filling the room that I was somewhat sure were coming from me.

"Let go, Sabrina," he growled, his head moving between my thighs as my hands scrabbled at the sheets. "Let go," he commanded again, and I did, an electrifying wave sliding through me as I cried out, the tension and release mounting and then cresting deliciously as I found Zane's head and held him there, right where I needed him to stay.

After a moment, he slid up my body, pressing into my side, and as I regained the ability to think, I registered the steely length of his arousal at my side.

"Do you have a condom?" I asked, suddenly able to think of nothing past feeling him inside me, giving him some part of what he'd just offered me.

A moment later, he was hovering over me, legs on each side of my thighs as I reached between us to notch the thick head of his cock at my entrance. Zane's dark gaze drilled into me with so much intensity I thought it was possible I might melt beneath him. I gripped him tightly, shifting my hips up to encourage him in, and then slid my hand around to pull him closer as he began to move. He inched himself forward slowly, so painfully slowly, that I was lifting my hips to meet him, to encourage him, crying out in frustration as he continued the controlled, measured invasion of my body.

His eyes never left my face, even as he pressed in fully, even as we began to move together, sensation rocketing through me as he thrust into me, over and over. He was beautiful to watch, all concentration and intensity. And when his steely intent began to dissolve, when his mouth opened and a guttural groan escaped as his arms tightened around me like steel bands, he was even more beautiful.

"Yes," I whispered, encouraging him to lose control, desperate to see it, to feel it. "Yes."

His body shuddered as his hips moved faster, harder into me, and just as he began to falter in coordination, I felt it—the jolt running through his body and transferring to mine, the pulse of him where we met, where he filled me. And the release, Zane finally stilling and then collapsing atop me with a shaky breath, our hearts hammering as one until he finally slid to one side, keeping me close in his arms.

"So," he murmured sleepily. "I haven't read the official guide, but I'm ninety-nine percent certain roommates aren't supposed to have sex."

I opened my eyes to look at him, relieved to see a sleepy smile on his handsome face. "I don't think either one of us is known for following rules," I said.

"True," he agreed. And soon, his breathing steadied, and I lay in Zane's arms, trying to decide what might happen next.

I was only sure about one thing. That I'd just given my body and at least part of my heart to someone who wasn't planning to stay. That once again, I'd chosen someone who wouldn't choose me.

# Chapter Eleven

## Zane

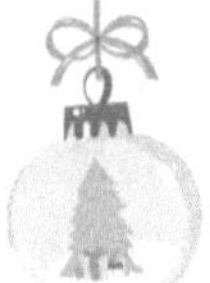

Sabrina was everything I'd imagined. Soft and tender, fierce and demanding. And having her in my arms, touching her, hearing her cry out—it had been so much more than my imagination was capable of inventing.

I woke the next morning with Sabrina pressed to my side, her dark blue hair adorably messy and one of her hands pressed up under her chin. She looked almost childlike, sleeping so peacefully in the circle of my arms. But my mind flashed continually on memories from the night before, when she was anything but childlike.

I thought I might stay in bed with her all day, but my phone buzzing on the nightstand pulled me away, and I opened my texts to find the real world inserting itself into our happy cocoon.

Two texts waited for me, each from steady clients in Denver.

They had new commissions, work for new developments in Lakewood and Brighton. Big jobs that I needed to take on to keep my business going. Big jobs that I couldn't do here.

I sighed and rolled out of bed.

"Hey," Sabrina said, the sleepy rasp of her voice nearly pulling me back in beside her.

"Hey," I said, sitting back down, letting one hand find her form beneath the covers so I could trace the shape of her.

"Everything okay?" She asked, her brow furrowing.

"Yeah. Just need to get to Dad's shop and see what kind of materials he has. I might need to start some work for a client back at home."

She nodded, then sat up. "You need your bike."

I'd forgotten about that. "Ah, yeah. I do."

"Give me ten minutes," she said, and a moment later she was sliding from my bed, her gorgeous naked form crossing my floor and leaving the room. I heard the bathroom door click shut in the hall, and did my best to pull my mind from the thought of her beneath me, the delicious feel of her around me.

Unfortunately, the only other thoughts I had to turn to were much less pleasant. There was Dad, and then there was my business. I'd need to go spend some time with Dad today, and then I'd need to make a plan for the commissions my clients were looking for. Metal craft, unfortunately, was not a mobile career choice. The work I did often required most of the space in my warehouse, since I was often creating gates and railings, and other big things that took up space—and were nearly impossible to ship.

As I pulled on a pair of jeans and ran my hands through my hair, I tried to mentally arrange the calendar that lived in my head. How long would I need to be here for Dad? How soon could I get back to Denver? And why did that thought suddenly evoke a completely different set of emotions than it had just a few days ago?

I knew the why of it.

I just didn't know what to do about it.

"Ready?" Sabrina asked, meeting me at the door.

"Yeah."

Sabrina was fresh and beautiful, wrapped in a soft-looking blue sweater and faded jeans. We headed out to her car, and all I wanted to do was head back into my room with her and forget the real world for a little bit longer.

"Everything okay?" she asked as she guided the purple pickup through the streets of Holly Creek, which were quiet and still in the November chill. A layer of frost coated everything, and the cars parked in front of the shops seemed to gleam and sparkle.

"Yeah," I said. She didn't need to know the mental gymnastics I was going through.

Sabrina pulled up behind my bike, and I hesitated, not eager to ride through the frigid wet air or to leave the intimate warmth of the truck. "What are you up to today?" I asked, picking up my helmet from the seat between us.

She scratched the back of her neck and her big green eyes found mine, widening as she spoke. "I'm supposed to be signing the lease on the second location today."

"Supposed to be?"

She huffed out a little breath. "I mean, I am. I think. I—"

"Why aren't you sure?"

"More time, more responsibility, more... risk."

I looked down at the helmet in my lap. That made sense. "I get it." I lifted my gaze to meet hers. "But there's hardly ever reward without risk. And at least you're considering it before you take action. That's pretty much the polar opposite of the way I've done everything in my life."

She smiled, making me feel like I'd won some kind of award for being clever. God, I loved her smile.

"You're more of a jump first, check the chute later kind of guy?"

"That makes it sound far more planned out than my life ever actually is," I said. "I'm more of a desperate action followed by equally desperate accounting for that action kind of guy."

She tilted her head, her brows lowering. "Example?"

"Going to Denver. I knew one person there—my cousin, but when I left here I was so desperate to get away, to get anywhere, I headed straight there."

"And it worked out."

"Luckily it worked out." It had been luck. My cousin Sandro had been a good friend in childhood—one of the only ones I'd had. But that didn't mean he was going to welcome me into his new life across the country. Still, he had.

"And what else?"

"My shop. I started working for someone else, and he was defaulting on his loan. I took it over, having no clue if I'd be able to make it work."

"But you did."

"I did." It hadn't been easy, and margins were still pretty thin. But I'd made it happen. Talk of the shop reminded me that I needed to go attend to business. "Hey, I need to run. But you'll do the right thing. You'll feel it in your gut. And you can figure out the rest later."

She laughed, stirring desire inside me again, making my blood warm with the desire to touch her, hold her against me. "Thanks for the pep talk."

"Any time."

"See you tonight?" There was a definite note of suggestion in her voice.

"Definitely." I pushed open the door and stepped out to the curb, the bracing cold making it easier to focus on what I needed to do. "Bye."

"Goodbye, Zane." She smiled as I closed the door, and I tried to capture that image to hold in my mind all day.

Dad's shop was freezing that morning when I stepped inside and got the lights up. I adjusted the thermostat, but after an hour the needle hadn't moved. The action of moving helped a bit, and so did the welding I was doing to finish up a door grate that Dad had left unfinished.

I added broken thermostat or heater to my list of things to do.

I'd determined that one of my Denver clients didn't need me to start until January at the earliest, but the other needed a finished railing for a staircase by Christmas. Dad had the equipment I needed and I could buy the materials out here. But there was the not-small issue of getting a finished piece of heavy metalwork back to Colorado without spending the profit and then some.

I could ask John to get it started, but he was really a functional welder. The detailed stuff—the art, I guessed—was all me. When I couldn't put off making a decision any longer, I cleaned up the shop and went upstairs to talk to Dad.

"Hi there," Valerie said, greeting me as I came through the door. Dad was nowhere to be seen, and she saw me looking for him. "Ben is taking a nap."

"Ah." I checked my watch. It was eleven o'clock in the morning. "Was he up early?" I remembered Dad being up all kinds of crazy hours when I was a kid. Sometimes he'd be coming back in from working downstairs when I was just getting up for school.

"No," she said, and I heard a note of hesitation in her voice.

I went to the kitchen and made a cup of coffee. She stood in the doorway. "How's he doing?" I asked.

"Moving pretty slowly," she said. "I think it frustrates him."

"Sounds right." I poured cream into the dark liquid and breathed in the nutty scent. "How long until you think he'll be back to where things were before the heart attack? Or is..." I trailed off and faced her, sipping from the mug, which had a picture of a little cat in some kind of wheeled contraption and read "Half Cat Distillery" across it.

She shook her head. "I'm not sure that's going to happen, Zane. Your dad says he's been slowing down for a while. The heart attack was pretty serious—it may be a decline he doesn't come back from. Not all the way. Plus, the dementia..."

Her words made sense, the dementia was the thing I had a hard time getting my head around. I knew Dad couldn't work. It was clear he'd been dropping balls for a while now. Plus the sheer physicality of the job, and the inherent danger of the tools involved. If he wasn't tracking... I scratched my jaw. I'd known all this, but realized I'd been holding out some unrealizable hope. "I'm not sure what to do."

Valerie gave me a sympathetic frown. "It's not for me to say, but I'd think about closing up the shop for good. Unless you're going to stay to run it, or if your dad has a trusted employee who might take over. Or maybe to sell it to?"

"It's just Dad." I pictured him in the shop downstairs, where he'd always been. That was where he belonged, wasn't it?

"I'm sorry. This is hard." She did look sorry. I guessed this wasn't the first conversation like this that Valerie'd had, given her line of work.

I nodded, though everything inside me was fighting this idea. Dad wasn't an old man—at least not in my mind. And I'd spent so little time with him in the past years that my memory was likely supplanting the reality of him with my version of him. Steely and fierce, angry, and sometimes cruel. That Dad didn't become an old man who took naps at eleven in the morning. That Dad didn't lose track of what he was supposed to be doing. Did he?

"Sorry, I..." I glanced up at Valerie, who was watching me expectantly. "I guess I just hadn't understood the reality of this. I figured I was just here to close the gap until he got on his feet again."

"I get it. It's hard to see our parents aging." She touched my arm, offered a kind smile, and then turned. "I'm just going to go check on him."

"Sure," I said, leaning back against the counter with my cup between my palms, working hard to wrap my mind around everything. But it wasn't like he was gone. I couldn't make decisions on his behalf. I needed to talk to my dad.

# Chapter Twelve

## Sabrina

"All yours," my new landlord said, dropping the keys into my palm for my second location. "I can't wait to see what you do to it!"

"I'm hoping to be open by the beginning of December," I told her, squeezing the sharp edges of the keys against my palm in an effort to make it feel more real. I'd really done it. I'd taken a chance, decided that the risk was worth the reward.

Maybe Zane had made me brave.

But I liked to think instead that the best relationships just revealed the valuable qualities locked inside the participants. And Zane made me feel brave. And ready for a change.

If I could get this place up and running—which I was pretty sure I could—I'd bring in a second manager and spend my time worrying about high-level issues like bookkeeping and inventory. I'd delegate the day to day, and hopefully have more time for other things.

Things, my brain suggested, like rolling around in bed with Zane.

It had been hard to stay focused as I'd done the final walk-through of the new location. My body and my mind were solely fixated on the events of the previous evening.

Zane surprising me by setting me up with him. Having dinner together in the quiet corner of the restaurant. Spending the rest of the night learning what he liked as he did the same for me beneath the soft duvet of his bed.

Once the landlord had departed, I climbed up onto the counter, letting my legs swing down as I dialed Anya's number.

"Did you do it?" She sounded almost as excited as I felt.

"I did. I am sitting in the second location of Brewed Awakening right now!"

"Oh, I'm so proud of you! Good job, Sabby!"

"Anya, I did something else too."

There was a pause, then she said. "Why did your voice get all low and breathy when you said that? I hope you're not taking me up on that thing I said about helping you hide bodies. That was hyperbole."

"No," I laughed, glee swirling through my limbs as I watched the foot traffic pass by in the pale sunshine outside the windows of my new shop. "I did something else. With Zane."

"Wait, the hot roommate Zane?"

"Do you know a lot of Zanes, Anya?"

"Please tell me you're not going to let me down when I ask what the 'something else' is. Please tell me you didn't start some new hobby or something boring," she whined.

"Kind of a new hobby maybe," I said, thinking about all the different ways I'd like to do what we'd done the night before. Sex could be a hobby, right?

"Nooo... wait. You're making a joke. Your new hobby is a sexy hobby, right?"

"Yes."

There was a loud squeal on the receiver that forced me to hold my phone farther from my head. I switched Anya to speaker and held the phone in front of me. "That's amazing. Good for you. Yes. Good." As she said affirmative words, her voice lost emphasis until the last "good" did not sound especially good.

"Yes," I confirmed. "Good."

"Only..." Anya hedged.

"Not sure I want to hear it," I told her, the glee inside me sliding to a stop as it waited to hear whatever harsh reality Anya was about to point out that would surely tamp it down.

"I'm just...I worry about you."

"I'm a grownup. Just like you. We're the same age, remember?"

"I know, honey. Just...is he staying? Isn't he from like, California?"

"He's from here," I said, purposely missing the point.

"Right. Okay. Well, good. That's great."

I sighed. The excitement and happiness inside me had simmered down to a low level, tempered with a healthy dose of concern now, thanks to Anya.

"It is." I knew what she was getting at, and I knew she'd point it out.

"But he doesn't live here, does he? Like, permanently."

And there it was. "No."

She inhaled sharply and then her voice turned all false perky. "People make long distance work all the time, Sabs. It'll be fine. Or maybe was it just a romp?"

"I don't know yet." I hadn't analyzed it. I had only wanted to share my excitement. Now I regretted sharing anything.

"I should go," I told her.

"I'm so happy for you. We'll celebrate the new place. When will it be open?"

"If I work hard and get some hiring done quickly, a few weeks. By December."

"Amazing. Okay, well, enjoy this victory. And let's do champagne on Friday."

"Sounds good."

We hung up and I stared into the space around me, trying to imagine it with comfy couches and tables, customers working and talking, a cabinet full of snacks and the sound of the coffee machines whirring and steaming. It was going to be great.

And things with Zane? That was going to be great too. I let myself focus on the facts instead of the what-ifs swirling through my mind. The facts were clear enough. He'd chosen to meet me for dinner. He'd decided to be my date. And then he'd taken me home and spent the night being sweet and sexy, and perfect.

We'd figure the rest out later.

Still, I had a niggling sense of disappointment and I wanted to banish it, to enjoy my accomplishment. I dialed a familiar number, my mood immediately lifting when my brother answered on the second ring.

"Sis!"

"Hi Peter! Am I catching you at a bad time?" Peter was a lawyer, so it seemed like he was endlessly busy.

"Nope, not at all. How are you? What's new?"

"A lot, actually... I just signed a lease on a second location!"

"I don't remember reviewing a lease for you." He sounded only mildly perturbed.

"It was a simple lease. I'll send you a copy. Plus, my best friends are lawyers too, remember?"

"I don't mind, Sabrina..."

"I know, but we're actually the same age and sometimes I like to do things on my own."

"Yeah, we know." Peter's current irritation was mostly pretend, but it didn't erase the years the rest of my family had spent trying to get me to move back closer to home. "Does Mom know?"

"That I didn't ask you to look over the lease?"

"No. About the second shop. It pretty much means you're never coming home."

"Peter. I am home."

He was quiet for a long beat. "You sound happy."

"I am."

"Then I'm happy for you." I heard him take a sip of something, coffee, probably. He drank coffee all hours of the day and night. "I had a dream about you last night. I guess this is why."

"Was the dream about me getting keys or something?"

"No, you were riding a unicorn into a really important meeting. Very embarrassing, actually. But I always dream about you when you're making big choices in your life." He'd told me that before. It was part of our weird twin connection, I guessed.

"Sorry for interrupting your dream meeting with my mythical steed."

"No worries," he laughed.

"How's Charlotte?"

"She's great! Come visit soon, okay?"

"I will. Or maybe you guys can come celebrate the opening of the second shop in December?"

"Send me dates. We can try! I think we might make it to Anya's for Thanksgiving. Mom and Dad are taking that cruise, and everyone else is doing that crazy hike..."

"Oh yeah!" Half of my siblings were nutty outdoor types and they'd all signed up for a Thanksgiving West Coast something-or-other when Mom and Dad had announced their plans to take a cruise. Peter's job meant he couldn't go, but part of me thought he stayed for me. "Good, I'll see you there then." Peter and Anya had become friends almost as soon as I'd met her—they bonded over boring lawyer stuff.

"Okay."

"Thanks, Peter. Love you."

"Love you too, sis,"

When I got home that night, Zane was waiting.

The smell of pasta and meat sauce wafted through the back door as soon as I opened it, and a barefoot Zane stood in front of the stove holding a wooden spoon.

"Hi." I could hear the enormous smile on my face in the lilt of my own voice.

"Hey." Zane looked uncertain, like he might step closer, but was holding himself back.

I closed the distance between us, raising on my tip toes to kiss his cheek. He wrapped an arm around my waist and pulled me against him, dropping his lips to mine.

"How was your day?" he asked, releasing me.

"Pretty good." I held up the new key to the second location. "I signed the lease."

"That's great," he said. "I'm making dinner." He waved the spoon toward the stove. "Should be ready in a few if you want to go put your stuff down, and then you can tell me about it."

"Wow, this is so nice." I carried my things to my room, thinking about how I could easily get used to this. I didn't mean to, but I even thought about how this might look in the future, if we were to get serious, maybe even get married.

"It was one night," I whispered, staring into the mirror over my dresser. "Don't get carried away."

It was hard not to, with Chelsea's wedding on the horizon. Though there was little to do at this point. Still, I had commitment, white dresses, and forevers on the brain.

"Hey Sabrina? Dinner's ready when you are." Zane's deep voice floated back to me, and I pulled my eyes from my own face. There was no point making this something it was not. Anya was right. I was not going to get carried away.

But I couldn't stop the flicker of hope that had lit inside me.

I wanted my happily ever after someday too. And so far, no

one had ever stuck around long enough to even be a candidate. No one ever chose me.

"I poured wine. It felt like we should celebrate," Zane said, waving me toward the table, which was set and held a bowl of steaming pasta with sauce next to a Caesar salad and a basket with garlic bread.

"This is amazing. Thank you for cooking."

He lifted a shoulder, taking his seat without meeting my eyes. But then, he lifted his wine glass toward me, and those dark soulful eyes found mine, sending a simmer of want through me. "Congratulations on signing your lease today."

"Thank you." I sipped my wine, letting the wonder of the evening sink in. Had anyone ever made me dinner like this before? I didn't think so.

"How was your day?" I asked. "How is your dad?"

Zane lowered the fork, which had been halfway to his mouth. "Yeah. I don't know. Better, I guess?"

"But...?"

"I'm going to have to make some decisions. He won't be able to keep the shop running."

"Oh, I'm sorry."

"I'm noticing things, like the heater in there isn't working at all. That's not the kind of thing Dad would have ignored. He has a few jobs that are way overdue, too. Things were late before the heart attack."

I wasn't sure what to say to that. Zane looked so sad I wanted to reach across the table and touch him. "Ah. That must be hard."

He scrubbed a hand across his jaw. "Yeah. It's just... It's weird. I never thought I'd come back here, you know?"

"I can't imagine..." I couldn't. What would it feel like coming home after being driven away? "Is your dad at all grateful you're here?"

"He seemed like it at first. But now, I get the sense he'd like me to disappear again."

"Did you guys talk a lot while you were away?"

"I called him at Christmas, mostly."

"That was it?" I shook my head. I didn't see my family a lot—Mom wasn't a fan of my blue hair and I was tired of explaining it—but I talked to her on the phone every week. And Peter and I talked at least once a week too. My other siblings were less regular, but they all inserted themselves into my life routinely, which actually felt nice at this point. For years, I'd struggled to find an identity among a group of people who all seemed perfect while I just never quite found my rhythm. When I started getting tattoos and piercings, Mom suggested it was a bad way to get attention, but with brothers and sisters who were all perfect, it was one of the only ways I could stand out. Now, my looks were just who I was, but Mom still complained.

"Yeah. We haven't been close since Mom died." Zane gave me a look then that felt a little like a challenge.

"I'm sorry," I said. "That must have been really hard."

The steel left his gaze. "It was. At first. I got used to it. I kind of had the sense he always resented me, anyway."

I nodded, taking another bite of the pasta Zane had made. It was incredible, and I let my eyes slide shut as I chewed and thought about how hard Zane's life must have been.

When I opened them again, Zane was watching me, and something in his expression had shifted, becoming predatory and sharp. "Good?" It was practically a growl.

"So good," I said, my voice a breathy whisper full of suggestion.

Two seconds later, Zane was on his feet, taking my hand and pulling me from my chair. I threw my napkin to the ground and followed him toward his bedroom. Before we got there, he spun me around and stepped close, pressing my back into the wall in the hallway. His eyes burned into mine, setting every nerve ending inside me on fire. And then he was on me, hands, mouth, every part of him touching, teasing, devouring me.

We didn't make it to the bedroom. Instead, I pulled at his jeans until he unfastened them and he peeled off my pants, dropping them in the hallway. We were a heaving jumble of hands and limbs and heat, and so much want, and after he rolled on a condom from his wallet, Zane took me there in the hallway. Against the wall.

Every thrust had me moaning like women I'd seen only in movies, but there was something so hot about the entire situation, and the position had him touching something inside me that was like a spark just about to set the whole house on fire.

Zane held me up, my legs wrapped around him, and the way his arms flexed as he held me while he pumped into me had me practically out of control with my desire for him. To have him on me like this, in me, wanting me so much that he couldn't wait until we were in bed.

I loved every second of it. And when he shifted slightly, whatever new position he'd found sent me right over the edge, not caring what kinds of sounds I might be making as I came.

He followed me there, grunting through a release that sounded every bit as powerful as my own, and then he wrapped me in his arms, cradling me as he walked me to his bed and carefully laid me down. Zane climbed on beside me after a quick trip to the bathroom, wrapping me in his strong arms.

"Wow," he whispered against my neck.

Yes. Wow.

I let my eyes slide shut, enjoying the feeling of him here, of having him want me like this. And on the screen inside my mind, I tried very hard not to project too far into the future. But words like "stay" and "forever" were flickering through that verdant hopeful space.

They were only words. They didn't mean anything.

# Chapter Thirteen

### Zane

What was I doing?

That was the question that kept going through my mind as I watched myself, as if from above, encouraging Sabrina. Which wasn't exactly the right way to describe what was happening. I was encouraging myself, telling myself it was okay, that I could have things and still walk away.

Only, I didn't want to walk away from Sabrina.

But I couldn't stay in Holly Creek.

As we lay in bed that night after actually finishing dinner and then ending up in Sabrina's room for round two, my mind was peacefully blank.

"You know, my best friend went to high school with you," she said quietly.

High school. One of my least favorite subjects. "I wasn't a happy person in high school."

"She says you were a hot loner."

Apt. "Sounds right, I guess. The loner part."

"Do you remember Anya Griffen?"

I did. "Pretty. Cheerleader."

Sabrina laughed, a breathy, sexy sound that had my arms

tightening around her without me telling them to. "Yeah. It's hard to imagine her as a cheerleader, but she was. She's a lawyer now. And a mom. She was one of the first people I met when I came to town and took over the shop."

An answer didn't feel required so I stayed silent, letting her talk.

"You were never really happy here." It was a statement, but I could feel the question in it.

"No."

"So it's pretty unlikely that you'd want to come back. Like... to stay."

I felt my body stiffen. The idea of coming back here permanently was something I'd considered vaguely, but not in any real way. I had a life back in Denver. Kind of. I had a business and a home, at least. "Pretty unlikely."

She nodded against my chest, but I felt the mood shift in the room. Between us. What were we doing, anyway? "Any chance you're staying long enough to be my wedding date?"

"When's the wedding, again?"

"Christmas. The twenty-third. In New York."

For a second, the thought of taking Sabrina to New York City sounded better than anything in the world. But then I considered the circumstances. A tux. A fancy party. I was about to say no, but I tilted my chin down and looked into those eyes again, and it was over. "Sure."

"You will?" She sounded like she didn't believe me.

"Yeah," I said, slowly realizing that I'd just committed to staying here another month. "I might need to go home first, but I can come back for it. I should see Dad at Christmas anyway."

Her face fell a little, but she covered quickly. "Right. Okay."

She nestled against me for a few moments more, but things didn't regain the warm comfort they'd held prior to the conversation about me in Holly Creek. About me staying.

"I should probably go back to my own room," I said, beginning to slip out from beneath her.

She sat up and stared at me, those green eyes like lasers, boring through me. "No, it's fine. You can stay."

"I just..."

"You don't want me to get the wrong idea and get all clingy or whatever."

"No, it's—"

"Zane," she said, her face tightening so I couldn't see what she was really thinking or feeling. "I can do casual. I know you have no intention of staying here, so I don't want you to think I've made this into something it's not."

Why did those words carry a sting with them? "Okay."

She nodded as if we'd decided something, but I was still sliding from the bed, gathering my jeans from the floor.

"I'll, uh... see you tomorrow." I left, closing the door behind me and focusing on getting into my own room, getting some sleep.

I was not going to think about the way Sabrina's words had unlocked something I'd been refusing to feel, some quiet glimmer inside me that had begun to glow just a little brighter when she was around.

The next day, I was in Dad's shop early in the morning, finishing up the last of the work he'd left undone and making phone calls to try to resolve some of the issues his illness had created with customers.

"I'm just not sure I should be paying for something that's being delivered four months late, son." Jesse Temple was on the other end of the line, making perfect sense. And his was not the first account this morning to question my assertion that his invoice was past due.

"I understand that," I said, repeating the conversation I'd had at least ten times now. "And I'm happy to give you twenty percent off for the inconvenience."

"I'll pay half," he said, his voice flat.

"Done."

I'd barely recouped fifty percent of the outstanding invoice amounts Dad was owed. Part of it was the jobs he dropped when he had the heart attack, but there was work here from before that.

At this point, even with fifty percent of the outstanding receipts coming in, I didn't have enough to keep the place running. I stood in the center of the concrete floor, looking around at the machinery and scrap that had been the background for most of my childhood. There were a few things I might keep, but I'd need to sell the rest, I knew. And it probably wasn't worth keeping old equipment and shipping it to Denver. It'd be cheaper and smarter to buy new things there if I needed them.

I ran my hand along a table I remembered sitting under as a kid, listening to the music Dad played while he worked, my nose itching with the smell of ozone, even as the fans ran and the garage door was rolled all the way up. I should never have been there—no kid of mine would be exposed to the fumes created while welding. But Dad didn't know about that. Or maybe he didn't care.

But I knew that wasn't true. He did the best he could. For a while at least.

I cleaned up the shop. Now that the outstanding jobs were done and Dad wasn't going to be taking on anything new, there was no point delaying the inevitable. I needed to sell the place. Or just close it down.

I squeezed my eyes shut and shook my head. A couple more days wouldn't hurt.

Upstairs, Dad was playing cards with Sophia.

"Hey," I said, stepping into the apartment.

"Hi Zane," Sophia said, lifting her head to shoot me a friendly smile.

"Son."

Dad held a fan of cards in his hand, and he was frowning at them as if they'd disappointed him. I poured myself a cup of coffee and watched, leaning against the counter in the kitchenette.

"You just ask me about something you have in your hand," Sophia said, her voice light and full of humor.

Dad shot her a quizzical look, and then went back to frowning at his cards. "Eight."

"No eights here. Go fish, Ben." Sophia pointed at the pile in the middle of the table.

Dad frowned at it again, and then glanced up at her.

"You get to draw a card. Maybe it will be an eight."

He took a card and turned it face up on the table. "Not an eight."

"That's okay. You put that one in your hand now too. You can ask me about that card on your next turn."

Dad's frown grew deeper, and he shook his head. He laid down the cards on the table and stared at them for a long moment. Then he lifted his eyes to Sophia. "Sorry, darlin'. This game is just a little complicated, I guess."

"That's okay, Ben. Another time."

Dad was already shuffling back to his bedroom.

"See you later, Dad," I said.

"Zane."

He disappeared through the doorway, Sophia at his back. I stared at the cards, finishing the stale coffee as I waited for her to return.

After a few moments, she did, a light smile on her face. She picked up the cards on the table, tucking them back into the box. "How are you doing, Zane?"

"Dad can't play Go Fish?"

She put the cards down, her eyebrows lifting at my tone. "He gets confused pretty easily. I'm guessing that was happening before the heart attack?"

"I wouldn't know." Guilt edged in around the resentment I'd always felt for Dad. I hadn't been here. I didn't know he was struggling.

She nodded her understanding.

"So he, uh... he's not going to suddenly get better, is he?"

She lifted a shoulder. "That's not the usual progression, no."

It was like I needed to keep hearing it in order to really believe it.

"I'm gonna need to talk with him about some things," I said, thinking out loud more than anything else. "The shop downstairs. Where he'll live..."

She nodded.

"And I need to get back home soon."

"I understand," she said. "It's hard living far away and having a sick parent. If there's anything I can do for you, we're here to help you, too."

"Thanks. Just knowing you're here is a big help." And it was. I couldn't imagine being the one to be here with Dad all the time. Maybe if he didn't seem to hate me, but even then. There was too much between us now to just move on.

I had a lot of thinking to do.

Downstairs, I climbed onto my bike and set out, no real destination in mind, no plans forming in my mind.

The only thought I could find that felt right was Sabrina.

# Chapter Fourteen

## Sabrina

We were just getting ready to close up when I heard the rumble of a motorcycle at the curb, and looked outside to see Zane pulling up. My heart hadn't gotten the memo, evidently, because despite the fact I'd spent the entire day reminding myself that this was a fling, that he was not a permanent fixture in Holly Creek, it was beating wildly as he approached the door of the shop.

Trent was at the door before I could get there, ready to tell him we were closed, but just as he swung open the door to meet Zane, I stepped near.

"Hi there, we were just closing up," Trent said with a kind smile.

"It's okay, Trent. This is my roommate Zane."

Zane's eyes glanced off Trent's face and held on mine, the deep, dark depths of them pulling at things inside me that were hardly coffee-shop appropriate.

He gave Trent a nod, and as my new manager headed back behind the counter to finish closing up, I took in the rest of Zane's appearance. He looked tired, a little drawn even. And he had the glassy-eyed look about him that he'd worn that first night I met him.

"You okay?" I asked, stepping aside and ushering him in out of the cold.

He rubbed a hand through his hair in answer, shaking his head a little. "I've been riding for hours."

"Because..."

"Needed to think."

Something in his tense shoulders, the grim lines of his face, told me he needed more than a quick chat in the door of my shop. I turned back to Trent.

"You good to lock up?"

"I've been trying to get you to let me close up for a week now," he laughed. "So yeah. Go. I'll see you tomorrow. Early, since you won't let me open, either, and Paul's off." Trent chuckled as he practically shooed me out the door.

Zane and I fell into step along the sidewalk, and I pulled my coat close around me against the brisk November chill. Thanksgiving was this week, and it felt like winter was rushing in.

"Dinner?" I asked him, glancing up at the stoic face beside me.

He gave a brisk nod, and I led him into the quiet little restaurant two blocks down from my shop. It was Italian, and though the lights were low and the music was soft, it was less romantic than it was comforting. We were led to a corner booth and we settled in next to each other, silence dropping around us.

Zane stared at his hands on the table, and barely responded when the server came to offer us wine. I waited, and when we each had a big globe of red in front of us, I dropped my hand on one of his.

"Hey."

He raised his gaze slowly, and gave me a lazy smile. "I'm sorry. I know I'm like a zombie."

"A sad zombie."

"That's not a thing. Zombies don't have emotions."

I thought about that for a minute. "Do we know that?"

"Do we know anything about zombies, really?"

"Good point." I raised my glass and sipped, glad Zane seemed to be coming out of his catatonic state. "So..."

"Yeah. So."

He gave me a look that fueled the hope inside me that I'd been valiantly trying to douse. The hope that maybe there was really something here, that we had a genuine connection. I swallowed it down.

He shook his head, took a drink of his wine, and then cleared his throat. "I need to figure out what to do about my dad."

I nodded. This wasn't new, but the sadness on Zane's face was.

"I think today I just realized finally that he's not going to suddenly get better, curse me out, and let things go back to the way they were."

"Would you actually want that?" I couldn't imagine wanting to be told off by my dad. Sent away.

"It would be familiar at least."

"I guess." I sipped my wine and watched him, the dark eyes deeper and sadder than I'd seen them yet.

"He's just... he's not that guy now. And it's clear he's done working. So I need to sell the shop, I guess. Move him into some place we can afford... get back to work."

"Wasn't that kind of the plan?" We'd talked about this before. Maybe not in concrete terms, but I thought it was decided.

"Hard to accept, I guess. But yeah." He glanced up at me, then dropped his eyes again. "Part of me feels wrong leaving."

"Because your dad needs you."

Zane didn't answer immediately, but he bobbed his head silently, staring at the tablecloth. "Yeah, Dad. But also..." he paused, his eyes catching mine.

I held my breath, hoping he might say that he thought there was something worth exploring here. Between us.

"I don't know." It was like a door slammed shut. His eyes hit the table again, and my mood deflated.

But what did I expect? That he was going to say he wanted to stay for me?

I took a deep breath. "That's okay." I straightened my shoulders, attempted to turn clinical, remove my own emotion from the situation. "It's hard to see a parent change, to lose themselves. Especially with dementia."

"Right."

"So how can I help?" The question brought his eyes back to mine, and for the first time since he'd stepped off his bike looking lost, I felt like he focused.

"This helps, actually. Just hanging out." One side of his mouth lifted in a trial smile. "Thanks."

"If I could save the world by ordering a glass of wine..." I joked.

"You know what I mean. You. Being here. Listening."

I smiled, taking a sip of the dense berry-ripe wine just as plates of steaming lasagna arrived. "Well, what I can't fix, lasagna surely can." I was keeping it light. I needed to, for self-protection.

Zane watched me for a long beat after I said that, a flicker of emotion in his eyes I couldn't quite read.

"Better?" I asked him when his plate and the big glass of red wine were empty. His cheeks had regained some fullness, and his eyes had lost the haunted look.

That half smile lifted his mouth again on one side, and that tiny motion was so sexy, my whole body heated in response. The blush rushed up my neck and I dropped my eyes, reaching for my water glass.

"It wasn't just the food," he said, his voice low and deep. "It was the company." He waited, but I kept my gaze on my glass.

We weren't doing this, right? He was leaving. I needed to get on with my own life. We were roommates who'd agreed to go together to a wedding next month. That was all.

"Sabrina." The way he said my name had every cell in my body leaning toward him.

"Yeah," I said, dragging my eyes up to meet his.

"You're amazing." His eyes were molten, full of the same want I felt all the way to my core. "I wish we'd met somewhere else. At some other time. I just—"

"You're leaving."

His gaze held mine.

"Not tonight though."

I knew I shouldn't let myself fall deeper, but I couldn't stop it. I wanted him. Not just because he was singularly beautiful, but because something inside him clicked with something inside me. I felt it, and I was pretty sure he did too, but it would do neither of us any good to acknowledge it. The time and place were wrong.

But we had this moment.

We paid, and soon, we were outside again, fighting the chilling wind back down the sidewalk, Zane's arm around me as we huddled together. When snow began falling lightly just as we reached the truck, he grinned at me, and then looked around with wide eyes.

"Like magic."

"You must get plenty of snow in Colorado."

"This feels different." As he helped me into the truck, I sensed he was talking about more than the snow. "I'll follow you," he said.

I navigated the few blocks home, a warm anticipation building both inside my chest and in the small cab of the truck as I watched Zane in the rear view mirror, riding through the snow on his bike. Everything about being with him felt right to me, in a way no one else ever had.

But as he'd said... we needed to have met somewhere else. At some different time.

Zane parked under the shelter of the garage awning and came back to the truck door. "Come on." HIs voice was rough as he reached a hand in for me.

He tucked me into his side as we hurried through the snow scattering lightly around the walkway to the back door. I watched as Zane's strong artist's hand put the key into the lock and turned. So. Sexy.

A moment later, we were inside, and silence engulfed us. It wasn't awkward though, just tense and sharp. I took off my coat, hung it in the hall, and met Zane at the bottom of the stairs.

Neither of us said anything, but the look that passed between us might have singed the wallpaper a bit. I took his hand and pulled him up the stairs behind me.

At the landing, Zane tugged my hand, spinning me back into him. I lodged against the solidity of his chest and took a deep breath, looking for something strong inside me that would tell him no. If I took one more step into my bedroom, where I fully intended to take him, I had the sense that I'd be lost. I was hanging on to my common sense by the barest of threads as it was.

"Sabrina," Zane whispered my name in a voice like pure want, and it pushed me over the edge.

I pressed up onto my toes, my hands sliding up his chest as my eyes met his, and then I was lost. Our mouths crashed together as our hands pulled and grabbed at clothing, all while we moved as one being into my room. By the time the backs of my knees hit the bed, I was shirtless, Zane's mouth was on my neck, and my hands were pushing his jeans from his hips clumsily.

The duvet rushed up to meet me as I let myself fall backward, and Zane kicked off his shoes and pants, joining me a second later as I struggled to push off my own jeans.

"Mine," Zane growled, covering my body with his and taking over, strong hands gripping the waist of my jeans and his head following their progression down my body. He dropped them on the floor, standing before me at the foot of the bed, and I inhaled a sharp breath.

His tattoos snaked around his torso, the dragon's wing from his chest wrapping slightly to mark his neck. His body stood solid beneath the marks, muscle and skin and ... pure male. Everything inside me tightened in response. And when his dark eyes scraped down my body, I actually shivered.

"Come here," I suggested, aching for him in every cell of my body.

He did, slowly, sliding up my legs, trailing hot kisses along the side of my thigh until he reached that needy place between my legs, and he pressed my thighs apart roughly before looping them over his shoulders and tugging me down the bed.

"Oh!" His mouth was on me before I had a chance to register what was happening. Heat, suction, movement and desire spiked straight through me, and I wasn't sure in that moment what day of the week it was, or what my name might even be. I knew only the need and the man intent on fulfilling it.

Someone was chanting, "ohgod, ohgod, ohgod," and it was just becoming irritating when I realized it was me. The next second, Zane added a thumb to press on my center, and the chant erupted into a scream as the orgasm ripped through me.

Zane worked me through it, lightening his touch but never stopping, until the waves came softer and slower, and then he grinned up at me, wiping his hand across his mouth. Cocky. Pleased with himself.

He climbed to rest at my side, and as my strength came back to me, I became aware of the stiff, pulsing heat lodged against my thigh. Unbelievably, every bit of desire came rushing back through my veins, coupled with something much more frightening—the urge to take care of this man beside me. Here, but also out there, out in the world that had hurt him and betrayed him in the past.

I let my fingers play along his length, teasing, as I arched up to kiss him again. When his tongue met mine, I wrapped my fist around his cock, pleased at the groan he let go in response.

We shifted, and I rolled on top of him, breaking the kiss only to adjust my positioning and pull a condom from the bedside table. Then I was rolling it down his length as he watched with burning eyes, lowering myself onto him slowly as he gritted his teeth, and moving languidly as he hissed out a breath.

"You're killing me," he murmured, watching me move above him in what looked like fascination.

"Definitely not the objective."

"I'll die a happy man," he said.

I wanted him to be happy. I wanted to be the one making him happy. Not just now. But for the foreseeable future.

And as the thought came to me, I stilled. This. This was why casual sex with your roommate was a bad idea. I didn't do casual. And for me, it seemed like proximity—not absence—made my heart grow fonder.

As I increased my rhythm, feeling the pressure mounting inside me as Zane's body told me he was nearing the edge, I realized how truly screwed I was. I'd already started to fall for him.

And when we came, seconds apart as my world exploded from within and then reassembled itself in the shape of a hot, tortured, tattooed man who rode a motorcycle like some kind of sexy dark horseman, I decided there was no point trying to change things. I'd enjoy the time we had. I'd handle the fallout later. With wine and plenty of ice cream. But that was a problem for future Sabrina.

I rolled to one side of Zane, startled to see those dark eyes intent on mine.

"Deep thoughts?" he asked as he rolled away for a moment to deposit the condom in the trash can near the bed.

"Too satisfied for thoughts," I lied.

He pulled me into his side and sighed deeply. "I could get used to this, Sabrina. You're amazing."

I clung to those words like Leo and that door in the North Atlantic, knowing they weren't enough to carry us both. So when he offered more, it was like a lifeboat appearing on the horizon.

"I didn't expect to find you. Not here, like this. Maybe there's some way we can figure it out though? The distance thing?"

"Maybe," I whispered.

"Maybe," he agreed.

My mind spun, and I was about to ask for something more, something definitive, when Zane's phone rang from the foot of the bed, shattering the bubble we'd created.

"Shit." He scrambled for it, picking it up as I watched the muscles of his back flex under the ink. "Hello?"

The muscles tensed, and he was off the bed, pulling his pants back on with the phone held in one hand. "I'll be right there."

My heart sank as Zane finished dressing.

"I have to go. It's Dad." He turned to face me, his face like a slideshow of emotions. Then he glanced out the window. It had snowed. A lot. "Oh shit. I can't take my bike."

"Take the truck. I can walk to work if I have to."

He looked like he might argue, but then his shoulders slumped and he pushed a hand through the back of his hair. "Thanks."

"I think we left the keys on the counter in the kitchen."

He moved to the side of the bed, gave me a quick kiss, and then he was gone.

# Chapter Fifteen

## Zane

It was dark and cold on the streets as I navigated to the hospital, and the purple truck I drove felt like the only car active in a desolate and abandoned world.

My heart had already gone through multiple phases of pain —why were things so complicated where my dad was concerned?

The hospital glowed like a lantern against the deep darkness of the November night, and a strange calm engulfed me as I stepped through its doors, making my way to the front counter.

"Emergency," the woman at the front told me, her bright pink lipstick at odds with the quiet dignity of the hospital at night.

In the emergency department, I checked in with yet another desk. "Ben Crosby," I told the man there. "My dad. I think he's just arrived? Recently?"

I shoved a hand through my hair as the man consulted his computer screen, in no apparent hurry at all. How strange, I thought, to have a job that was so mundane and everyday to you when the content of your work was literally life and death.

"He's with the doctor now," the man told me. "If you'll have a seat, someone will come out to check in with you."

"Can I see him? He has dementia—I'm not sure he can navigate all this alone."

"He's with, um... Sophia? A nurse?"

That was something, at least. But still. "I'm his son."

"We only allow one person to be with the patient at a time. I'll have someone send Sophia out. Maybe you can relieve her."

A few moments later, the familiar redhead appeared in the waiting room, her kind eyes finding me. "Zane," she said, leaning down to embrace me where I sat. I half-rose, but she dropped into the chair at my side.

"How is he?"

"He's okay. Confused. A little frightened, but he'd never admit it."

"Right." I swallowed down the rush of emotion her words inspired. "What happened?"

"He got up in the middle of the night. I heard him, and went to help, but he became really agitated. I'm not sure if he was still dreaming, or..." she shook her head. "He didn't want me to help him."

"Was he just going to the bathroom?"

She shrugged. "He was really foggy. I'm not sure why he was up, but he kind of fought me when I suggested he go back to bed."

"Fought you? Like...physically?" I scanned her arms, suddenly worried Dad could have hurt her.

"I'm fine. But he kind of swung for me, and I backed up, and he fell. He hit his head on the door frame." She said this last part quietly, like maybe it was her fault.

"I'm so sorry that happened." I dropped my head into my hands. "You shouldn't have to—"

"Zane. It's okay. This is the progression. It's my job. But it does mean that we may be at a point where Ben isn't safe at home."

I looked up to find her kind eyes shining as she looked at me. "Yeah." I was out of time. I needed to admit that Dad wasn't getting better, there was no miracle on the horizon, only the things that needed doing. And I was the one who had to do them. "Yeah. I'll find a place."

"Holly Hills is really nice. I work with a lot of patients there."

I nodded. That was one of the places I'd found in my searches, and one of the brochures the doctor had given me. The research had also suggested that there was a chance Dad's veteran's benefits would pay for at least some of the cost. I was about to get good at paperwork, I realized.

"You should go be with him," Sophia said. "Straight back, third bay on the left."

I rose, thanked her, and went to see Dad.

The tiny, frail man in the bed on the left was a shock. How could this man fight anyone? Poor Dad.

My heart felt like a lead weight as I moved to his bedside. His head turned to take me in, and his eyes actually lit up as his mouth pulled into a smile.

"You came." He sounded surprised and relieved all at once. I had a startling sense of de ja vu. Did he not remember that I was here?

"Of course."

"But you live so far away." A dressing wound around his head, half obscuring one watery gray eye.

I nodded. "I do. You needed me, though."

Dad seemed to think about that, his lips moving as if he was going to form words that didn't come. He reached a hand up from beneath the thin sheet, and I took it, doing my best to take this moment for exactly what it was and to shed the resentment inside me over the years when he would never have held my hand, no matter how much I might have needed him. He needed me now, and I could let the past go and be a good man for him. For Mom.

Dad's other arm was wrapped in dressings, some kind of splint holding the lower part of his arm straight and obscuring his skin. I was about to ask Dad about it, but someone appeared at that moment.

"Hi there," said a doctor, stepping into the space.

"Hi. I'm Zane. Ben's son."

The doctor smiled and moved to Dad's other side. "I'm Doctor Toffer. Seems like Ben's had a pretty exciting night," he said, his easy manner calming the storm inside me a bit. "Wasn't quite sure where he was for a bit there, but you're doing okay now, Ben?" He smiled at Dad. "We're in the emergency room at the hospital, right?"

Dad looked around as if this was news to him.

"How is he?" I asked.

"Your dad took a pretty good tumble. We're going to keep him overnight to monitor that bump on his head."

I nodded, not sure what to ask.

"We're more worried though, about the wrist. It's a serious break, and in a younger man I'd send him to surgery, no question."

"But for Dad?"

"Anesthesia and dementia are not a good combination," the doctor said. "We start to look at alternate treatments when we can, but I'm worried he may not regain full use of that hand if we don't operate."

I stared at the bandaged hand, as if it could offer some thoughts.

"Is Ben left-handed?" Dr. Toffer asked.

I stared at him. "I actually don't know. I don't think so. Dad?"

Dad looked between us, seemingly unsure himself.

"Even if he is, I don't know how much it will affect him at this point, losing some motor functionality," the doctor said. "I think the best bet is to set it, let it heal as well as it can, and then bring in some occupational therapy to help him regain use."

I nodded. How was I supposed to make decisions like this? There was no question this was my decision to make. But it felt weighty. It was too much.

"I think you probably know best," I told the doctor.

"Does your dad live with you?"

"Um. No." I pushed a hand through my hair, a strange wash of guilt pouring through me. "I live out of state."

The doctor made a little clucking noise, like he was disappointed in me. "Okay. Well. Let's get your dad admitted and moved upstairs, and we'll go from there."

"Okay."

After the doctor had left, I turned back to Dad, who seemed to be asleep. I sank into the chair at his side, dropping my head back to stare at the ceiling. I needed to make some decisions. Right now.

"Zane," Dad's weak voice came to me through my haze of exhaustion. I sprang to my feet.

"Yeah? Dad?"

"Thank you for coming. For being here. I wasn't..." Dad's mouth worked on these words for a long beat, but the clarity in his eyes was surprisingly sharp. "I wasn't a good father to you. I know. I'm sorry."

"I..." I sank back down into the chair at his side. He wasn't wrong. But it was the first time he'd ever acknowledged that my childhood might have been less than ideal, thanks to him. "It's fine. Just get some rest, Dad."

"You're a good man, Zane. Not gonna pretend I had anything to do with it."

If Dad had leaped from the bed and done a quick boogie I wouldn't have been any more surprised than I was at the clarity and truth of his words. They were so out of the blue and out of the context of the painful relationship we'd built over decades that I had no response. I didn't have any practice responding to these kinds of words from my father, and so I sat there, painfully blank, my heart a wound inside me.

"Okay." It was all that came out in response. It wasn't the right answer, but part of me wondered what the hell I owed him after all these years. Did he deserve any more than that?

Fuck. My head was a mess. I leaned back into the chair and shut my eyes, trying to give my mind a chance to sort through all the things that had begun cycling like a low-speed tornado. Too slow to make progress, too fast to grab any one thing and hold it down, and utterly devastating no matter the speed of rotation.

Hours later, Dad was settled in a room, his arm newly set in an enormous cast, and I had begun to take action. The sun was up and it was a new day.

I called Holly Hills and set up a time to go tour the place and discuss the potential for Dad to go there when he left the hospital. He wouldn't like it, but I'd confirmed with the caregivers that it was the best plan. They couldn't care for him at home, not with the dementia advancing so rapidly. He needed to be in a place with safeguards built in so he was safe.

Then, with my heart sitting inside me like a cinder block, I posted advertisements for the shop on several trade sites I found, using photos I'd taken with my phone over the past weeks. Crosby Metalworks had been in business more than sixty years, with Dad's father starting the place back when he retired from his first job, and I hoped that history would carry some cachet.

Dad never considered another career.

And honestly? Neither did I, not that I had many options. I just hadn't been able to see my way to doing the thing I was good at with a man who seemed to believe I was good for nothing.

Dad slept most of the day, thanks to the pain meds they were giving him for the arm and the bump on his head. They didn't think he had a concussion, which was a blessing. I'd texted Sabrina as soon as they admitted him, to let her know I'd have her truck a bit longer, and now I needed to get it back to her.

The sun was sliding from the sky when I pulled up in front of Brewed Awakening, and the warm light from within lit the shop like a scene from a cozy movie. Sabrina and Trent were behind the counter, and I sat for a long moment watching as he said something that made her laugh, and her face broke into the beautiful smile that filled my dreams as she leaned forward slightly, giggling.

Sabrina.

My feelings for her had grown beyond my intent, and I wasn't sure what to do about it.

I knew a few things.

I knew I needed to get home and attend to my own business. John had been keeping the place up, and he'd started work on the December commission. He could continue day-to-day jobs, fixes and small things. But John wasn't equipped to handle the kind of work I'd begun to bring in. The kind of work I loved.

I knew it felt wrong to think about moving Dad into some unfamiliar place and then just leaving him there. It wasn't as if I'd been around for years, or like we were great friends. But he was my father, and despite the years I'd spent resenting him, his words from earlier were lodged inside me, spreading their message like a virus across the damaged plains of my soul. They didn't make up for anything. But just knowing that some part of my father knew he'd hurt me... it wasn't nothing.

And I knew I'd never meet another woman like Sabrina. She

was wild and free, but responsible and tenacious. The perfect blend of the rebel and the good girl. And her fierce intelligence and sweet understanding weren't something I thought I'd ever find again. Nor did I want to look. If I left her here... I thought I'd spend the rest of my life trying to fill the hole she made.

"Hey!" Sabrina leaned in the passenger side window, catching me deep in thought. I hadn't seen her come out of the shop, as my brain had begun trying to work through the multiple issues I faced.

"Hey," I said. "I thought you might like to have your car back at some point."

She smiled, and I saw a mix of sympathy and concern there. "You doing okay? How's your dad?"

I blew out a sigh and dropped my head for a second.

"That good, huh?" Sabrina opened the passenger door and got into the cab with me, scooting close on the bench seat.

"Are you done for the day?" I asked her.

"I can be. Trent is almost too on top of things."

"That's a good thing."

She nodded. "I'm going to start working at the other location right after the holiday."

Holiday? I stared at her. "What? What day is it?" It couldn't be December already. I'd been a mess, but not that much of a mess.

"Tomorrow is Thanksgiving. Shop's closed until Saturday."

I nodded. My meeting at Holly Hills was Friday, and now I understood why the woman on the phone had laughed when I'd suggested we meet Thursday.

"You going to see your family?" I asked her.

She shook her head. "Not this year. Peter's coming here, though."

"Your twin?"

She grinned. "Do you have plans, Zane? I didn't want to assume anything..."

I let out a hard chuckle. "Nope. Don't think there's a turkey in the Crosby family future."

Sabrina had taken my hand and now she laced her fingers through mine. "There can be," she said lightly. "Would you spend the holiday with me? And my brother? We're going over to Anya and Alex's house, and you're definitely invited."

I didn't want to admit how much the invitation meant to me —I'd never cared about traditions or holidays. Or I'd been trained not to. Dad and I didn't celebrate things. Ever, really.

"I'd love that," I told her.

"Good. Then there's definitely a turkey in your future, Mr. Crosby!"

I leaned in and kissed her then, unable to find words that would make sense of the disorder inside me. The only thing that felt clear to me was this. Us.

We drove to where my bike was parked, and then home.

And after a quiet dinner where I told Sabrina what was going on with Dad, we went to bed in her room. I wanted to feel her close to me, to make her happy, to please her. But once her soft body was pulled in close to me, exhaustion won out.

As I drifted to sleep, Sabrina in my arms and the heavenly scent of her all around me, I heard her whisper, "Sleep well, Zane."

It was odd, but I'd never felt so safe in my life.

# Chapter Sixteen

## Sabrina

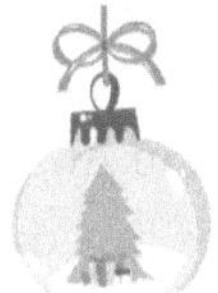

I was in charge of cranberries, and Zane went with me to the grocery store first thing in the morning.

As we stepped into the frantic space, last-minute shoppers practically sprinting down the aisles, he went one way and I went another.

"Hey! Cranberries are here, in produce."

He looked confused and pointed to an end cap where there were cans of pumpkin and canned cranberry sauce. "Cranberry sauce. Says it on the can."

"I was going to make it from scratch. It's really easy."

He frowned. "I buy this every year."

Something about the way he said it was both wistful and sad, and my heart tried to melt a little despite the stern talking-to I'd given it about falling any harder for Zane.

"Okay, tell you what. Grab one of those and I'll still make mine. We'll just bring two options."

Zane grinned and grabbed a can, and then we snagged the last bag of fresh cranberries and a couple oranges before heading home to get ready.

There was already Christmas music playing on every single radio station, and I was completely there for it.

"Isn't it a bit early?" Zane asked, watching me boil the cranberries with sugar and orange zest as sleigh bells rang and I sang along to every single song.

"Yes. But Christmas makes me happy."

"It isn't Christmas, though."

I turned to point at him with my wooden spoon. "Thanksgiving is merely the food-fueled gateway to Christmas. And in this town? Christmas started in August. You must've noticed."

"I remember." He said this in a dark voice and I glanced over my shoulder at him again as I stirred.

"No. You can't not like Christmas. That's just not allowed. That's like kicking puppies. Or saying wombats aren't adorable."

"The hockey team?" Zane wrinkled his nose.

I was facing him now, pouring the sauce into a glass dish to cool. "Hockey? No. What?"

"I thought maybe you were talking about the Wilcox Wombats and didn't quite get why you were calling them cute. Hockey players are usually missing teeth."

I sagged against the counter. "There are definitely cute hockey players. But quit changing the subject. Why don't you like the holidays?"

He stood and pushed his can of cranberry closer to the glass dish of sauce, as if reminding me that it needed to go too. "I just never had great holidays as a kid. And as an adult, do they really matter?"

"Um, yes they matter." My spine stiffened. "Holidays are a reason to celebrate a day that would otherwise be just like all the others. They're like magic, because everyone who celebrates does it on the same day, sometimes in the same way, and it's like this huge unifying event."

"Not for people who don't celebrate Christmas."

"True, but there are holidays of all kinds, all year long. This one is mine."

"Fair."

"And yours."

Zane made a non-committal noise in the back of his throat.

"Can we agree that we will celebrate eating too much and watching a parade today?"

"Um, okay. Parade?"

"And the dog show."

"Seriously?"

I nodded and told him, "Alex and Anya record both so we can watch them when we get there since they're on in the morning. "We'd better get going."

We'd agreed to stop by the hospital first, and I'd even talked Zane into letting me deliver some pumpkin muffins for his father, who I was a tiny bit nervous about meeting. Zane had explained that his father had been an intimidating force in his life as a kid, and the thought of meeting him felt scary. But important.

We drove to the hospital, and I did my best to shake my misplaced nerves. He was just a man. An old man. And though I knew he was old and sick, I wasn't quite prepared for the tiny man in the big hospital bed.

"Zane," he said, struggling to sit up when we entered the room.

"Hi Dad," Zane said, his voice less confident than I'd ever heard it. "Happy Thanksgiving."

Zane's father was reaching out a hand for him, and I watched Zane swallow hard before taking it and then turning to me. "Dad, I'd like you to meet Sabrina, my, uh... my roommate."

Mr. Crosby's eyes narrowed as he focused on me, and I steeled myself for a comment about my blue hair, or my tattoos. Instead, the thin mouth broke into a smile, and he said, "This is the first time Zane has ever brought a girl home."

"Hi Mr. Crosby," I said, laughing at the implication. "I brought you some pumpkin muffins." I set the muffins in the basket on the little table over his bed.

He turned his smile to Zane. "She can bake? Good job, Zane. She's a keeper." Ben Crosby had clearly chosen to skip right to the subtext, ignoring Zane's suggestion that we were just roommates. Or maybe it was obvious we were more?

Zane relaxed slightly, his shoulders losing the tension they'd held since we entered the hospital. He turned to me with a smile. "Yeah. She's pretty special."

We stayed for a half hour, Mr. Crosby clearly struggling to stay awake as we chatted about all kinds of things. My phone vibrated several times in my purse, but I didn't want to be rude. Finally, we said goodbye and headed back down to the car.

"Your dad was very nice," I told Zane.

"He was on his good behavior. Plus, you bribed him with food."

"Ha." I pulled my phone from my purse as we settled in the car to find at least seven texts from my brother.

Peter: We're here!

Peter: Where are you?

Peter: Charlie has taken one of my shoes hostage.

Peter: Are you ever coming?

Peter: You're missing the parade.

Peter: This kid has both my shoes now.

Peter: SABRINA!!


I laughed, showing the texts to Zane as we headed for Anya and Alex's house.

"Charlie has a thing for shoes?" he asked.

"I guess he does today. More to the point, Peter has a thing for kids."

"Oh yeah? I guess you guys had a bunch of siblings. That makes sense."

"Maybe," I agreed.

"Do you want a bunch of kids someday?"

I turned to see if the question came with any kind of expression that would tell me how Zane felt about that idea. "I don't know. A couple, maybe. But I really want to start with a dog."

"A dog, huh?"

"Something small." I wanted to ask how he felt about children, but we were pulling into the driveway already. Zane parked and came around to open my door and help me out with the sauces.

"There you are!" Peter's voice boomed through the house as we stepped inside, and in the next second I was swept off my feet and into my brother's arms.

"I don't know how you guys are twins," Alex said, taking the sauces from our hands as Peter put me down. "He's a giant and you're such a squirt."

"Squirt, squirt, squirt!" Charlie shouted, running straight into Peter's legs.

"Welcome to the madhouse," Anya said, taking my arm and smiling at Zane.

"Peter, I'd like you meet Zane. Anya, Alex, Zane Crosby." I did my best to make introductions, but Charlie was still yelling "Squirt."

"Come on. There's wine. It helps," Anya said, gesturing us into the living room.

The parade was on the television, and there was a warm glow in the room. The smells of dinner wafted around us, and happiness blossomed inside me. I took Zane's hand and pulled him to the kitchen to get a drink.

"Charlotte!" I greeted Peter's wife in the kitchen, and when she hugged me, I couldn't help the little yelp of joy that flew out of me. She was pregnant, and her tummy pushed up against me. "Why didn't I know?"

"Peter wanted it to be a surprise," she said. "Hello Zane, I'm Charlotte."

"Nice to meet you. Congratulations," Zane said.

"We're super excited," Charlotte said, and I tried not to feel hurt that Peter had kept this a secret. We were adults now. We had separate lives.

"I'm going to be an auntie!"

"You're already an auntie," Alex said, scooting past me to the oven with Charlie in her arms.

"Squirt!" My sort-of nephew yelled at me.

"I'm excited to be an auntie again," I assured her.

"You guys, this kitchen is too small to gather here, go watch the parade." Anya handed us wine glasses and sent Zane, Charlotte and I back to the living room.

The rest of the evening passed in a haze of wine and cheer and friendship and togetherness. I even caught Zane looking happy and relaxed as the recorded dog show came to a close long after we'd finished eating, despite his objections that the Irish Wolfhound was not nearly pretty enough to win.

"Majestic," Peter told him, repeating the announcer's proclamation.

"Right," Zane sighed.

"Hey," Peter said to me. "I'm stealing this guy for a minute. Go help the girls in the kitchen."

I frowned at him. "Sexist much? You go do dishes."

"I will be happy to in a moment. First I'm going to ask Zane about his intentions and then threaten him with castration if he hurts you even a tiny little bit. You want to stay for that?"

I glanced at Zane, who gave me a little shrug but didn't look worried. "Okay. No, I don't want to stay for that."

"Good. Go be womanly. Or if you don't want to wash dishes, ask if there's some wood you can chop or something. Whatever."

I rolled my eyes at Peter, but joined the ladies in the kitchen anyway. I hoped he wouldn't embarrass me too much with Zane. I'd had a feeling he'd say something after he'd caught the two of us kissing on the back porch just before dinner.

"Thanks for such a fantastic dinner," I said to my friends.

"It was amazing," Charlotte agreed. She perched on a stool at the counter. "Even if you won't let me help with anything."

"Not a chance," Anya said.

I helped put away some of the big serving dishes and silverware, and then we all took stools at the counter, steaming cups of decaf in front of us.

"Zane's getting the talk," I explained.

"Oh, the intentions toward my daughter talk?" Anya asked.

"Sister, but yeah."

Just then, loud laughter erupted from the front room.

"Sounds like it's going okay," Charlotte noted.

"Hope so," I said.

A little while later, we were saying our goodbyes, and I made plans to see Charlotte and Peter for lunch before they headed home the next day.

As we got into the car, I turned to Zane. "What did my brother say to you?"

"He told me I'd better take good care of you." Something burned in Zane's eyes as he looked at me across the console. "And that's exactly what I'm going to do when we get home."

He was as good as his word, but even as I dug my fingers into Zane's dark hair and rode through my second orgasm of the night, I realized that I still didn't know what might happen between us in the long term. Zane didn't live here. And no amount of fantastic sex or holiday dining would change that.

The next morning, I woke before Zane, and I spent a while in bed watching him and wondering if there was any way I might be able to keep him.

I didn't want to pressure him. I knew he was already under all kinds of pressure. If anything, I wanted to be an outlet, a way for him to relax through all the tough decisions he was having to make about his dad.

But I also didn't want to be left behind.

When his dad was settled and the shop was sold, what then?

Actually, I knew what. Zane would leave.

We'd had an expiration date going into this.

The very best possible outcome was that he'd be here through Chelsea's wedding in New York. And then he'd leave.

No matter how long it lasted, there was a broken heart waiting at the end of this for me.

Zane stretched and grumbled, and I slipped an arm around him, doing my best to push away the dark thoughts crowding my mind.

"Morning," he said.

"Good morning."

"Any day-after holiday traditions I need to know about?" He looped his arms around me and hauled me to lay on top of him.

The pressure of his body against mine helped push out the worries I'd been feeling, and a certain steely length against my thigh gave me an idea.

"There are, actually."

"Oh yeah?" he asked, those dark eyes meeting mine, sparks lighting within them.

"It's good luck to have sex the day after Thanksgiving. Everyone knows that."

"Huh. Never heard that one."

I nodded, pressing my lips into a line. "It's true."

"Well, I think I'm going to need some luck today..." Zane's hands found my ass then, and his mouth landed on my neck.

I positioned myself over the hard length of him and found myself moving rhythmically without planning to, the hardness of him hitting my clit in just the right way.

We didn't talk any more, just moved together, taking and giving what was needed. When I reached for the condom, Zane pulled me back on top of him, and I lowered myself onto his cock, every inch of it filling me in a way I didn't think I'd ever be lucky enough to find again.

Zane thrust up into me, but he let me drive the pace, and it was the best possible version of morning sex. Languorous and sleepy, hot and needy all at once.

And we both began the day with as much luck as was possible.

Soon after we rose, Zane kissed me goodbye. He was going to tour Holly Hills, the place he hoped his dad might live when he left.

And as I watched him ride away, I couldn't help feeling like it was the beginning of the end.

# Chapter Seventeen

## Zane

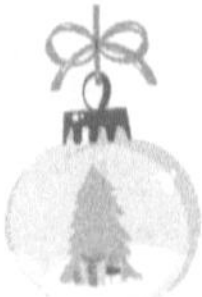

Dad resisted the move.

It was funny. He would forget that Mom was gone, somehow magically rewinding twenty years, but he still knew that he didn't live in the little one-bedroom apartment I took him to when he was released from the hospital a week after I'd toured Holly Hills and signed all the paperwork.

I'd spent the week in between moving as much of Dad's stuff as would fit into the tiny place, hoping to make it familiar and comfortable for him. But Dad tensed up the second I turned the wrong way out of the hospital parking lot.

"You lost, Zane?"

I chuckled, looking over at Dad in the cab of Sabrina's little truck. "Nope."

"Home's that way."

I sighed. We'd talked about moving. Multiple times. But I'd known somehow that it wasn't sinking in.

So the day was rough. Dad looking like a kid who'd been delivered to daycare and had no intention of staying through the morning. As I was puttering around his room, finding things to do so I could make sure he was really, truly, okay, one of the nurses knocked and then came in.

"Hi there. Welcome, Ben," she said, greeting Dad like she'd known him forever.

"Hey," I said, shaking her hand.

"You can tell this guy to go ahead and pack all that shit right back up," Dad told her. "I'm not staying."

I gave the nurse what I was certain was a look of exasperated desperation.

"Ben, I'll be right back. Do you want to say goodbye?"

I glanced at Dad. He did not want to say goodbye. "I guess I'll head out, Dad. I'll see you tomorrow, okay?"

Dad did not answer me, and I followed the nurse out the front door.

"This is completely normal," she started. "You're Zane, right?"

"Yeah." I rubbed a hand through my hair, which after two hours of Dad, I was pretty sure was already completely standing up.

"I'm Callie. This is hard, I know that. And it's definitely an adjustment. And this is going to sound completely bonkers, but with dementia patients, sometimes it's actually easier on them if family members don't visit for the first couple weeks."

"What? No, he'll wonder where I am—"

"He might. He might not. Most likely, his survival instincts will kick in and he'll settle. I've seen it hundreds of times. It will be much harder on you than on him."

That didn't feel right. Not at all. They'd mentioned this idea on the tour, but I didn't. like it. "I don't know. Our relationship is just starting to improve. If I abandon him—"

"Zane. You're doing the opposite. You're setting him up for success. You've brought him here. I know that wasn't an easy choice, but it was a good one. We're equipped to take care of him. And even if it doesn't feel like it, he is an adult. He will adapt. He's more resilient than you think he is. But if you come around every day, it will only make it harder for him. Give him a bit of time."

I stared at her. Her words made sense, but it felt wrong. "Will you call me? Let me know how he's doing?"

"Absolutely."

We exchanged numbers, and Callie promised to call me that night to report back.

I left, and drove back to the house, feeling empty and lost. Sabrina had gotten a ride to work with Paul, and I didn't want to go into the empty house alone. So once I parked, I walked the neighborhood, no destination in mind.

It was cold and windy, the sky looked like it really wanted to snow but couldn't quite get there, and the air around me smelled like wood fires. Despite the cold, I walked through the little neighborhood that had started to feel more like home than the loft I had in Denver.

The houses were each different, brick here, siding there. But each one had a distinct personality, like Sabrina's with its purple door and exuberant flower beds. People made lives in these little houses, I thought. Real lives. Where the other people in the houses mattered to them. Loved them.

I thought more about the empty loft back in Denver, the cold metal awaiting me in my workshop. I had to go back, that wasn't an option. But the idea had never held less appeal. Leaving Dad here like this... leaving Sabrina? They were both so alone.

Actually, as I considered, it wasn't that Sabrina would be alone. It was that I would be alone. She had family. She had friends. Sabrina had built a good life, and for a little while, I'd ridden her coat tails and enjoyed that life too. But it wasn't mine.

Me and Dad? Maybe we were just built to be alone.

The idea lodged in my chest but didn't sit comfortably there.

Still, I couldn't shake it, no matter how much I hated the truth of it.

It was in that state of mind that I stopped walking and turned up the front path of a little brick house probably a mile from the one I shared with Sabrina. A sign had caught my attention, and I went on instinct, making decisions with my gut.

I might regret it, but as I walked back to our house when I was done, I told myself that for once, I was just doing what felt right.

I picked Sabrina up from the shop when it closed at seven. I'd made dinner, and I was having trouble hiding the giddiness I felt at the other surprise waiting for her at the house.

"Why do you look like that?" she asked me. "All jumpy and weird."

"I always look weird."

"No. You always look hot and broody. Today you look hot and not broody. You look excited. Or worried. Or maybe nauseous. You okay?"

"Let's go back to the part where I look hot and just stay there."

"Hmm."

"Good day?" I asked as I drove back toward the house.

"Pretty good. I'm excited to get to the new shop next week and get it open."

I nodded. "Yeah. That's huge."

"How's your dad?"

I sighed as I guided the little truck up the driveway. "That was hard. I'll tell you about it in a minute... first, I have a surprise."

"That's why you look weird!" she laughed like she'd just solved a pressing mystery.

"Maybe, yeah. Come inside, but stay in the kitchen."

"Um, okay..."

I opened her door and led her into the house, closing the door behind her and then positioning her in front of it. "Eyes closed."

"Ookay," she said, shifting her weight impatiently. "Can I put down my bag or take off my coat?" She said this with her eyes closed, so I returned to her, taking her bag and helping her out of her coat before dropping a tiny kiss on her nose.

"Stay."

She giggled.

A moment later I returned, taking Sabrina's hand and placing it on the soft furry head of the surprise I'd brought for her.

She sucked in a sharp breath and said, "oh!" Then her eyes flew open, and she stared at the puppy in my arms, who was already gazing at her adoringly.

"Oh, Zane..." she didn't sound as excited as I'd hoped.

"You said you wanted to start with a dog." I pushed the fuzzy little thing toward her, and she took it in her arms, letting the dog's little snout push at her chin.

"I do, but... I don't know if I can handle a dog right now..." She nuzzled its nose and made a little "aww" sound under her breath, her eyes sinking shut.

"He can go to the shop with you. Keep you company."

"I'm not sure how the health inspectors would feel about that..." She stared at the puppy with adoring eyes.

My stomach was beginning to feel sick. This hadn't gone quite the way I'd planned. "I didn't think about that."

She dropped into a kitchen chair, holding the little dog on her lap and looking down at him wistfully, her fingers petting his soft little ear. He tucked himself into a ball on her legs and dropped his head. "Oh my god, he's perfect. But Zane, I don't think I can keep him."

I sat across from her, all the excitement and hope I'd felt earlier deserting me, leaving the uncomfortable truth I'd already realized sitting alone in the center of my mind. "Yeah. Of course not. I didn't think. That makes sense."

Her eyes jumped to my face. "You sound so defeated. I mean. I love him, I just..."

"It's okay. It was a stupid impulse."

"No, it was sweet. It's just...with the new shop and everything, I'll be working more than normal, and I can't take care of a new puppy..."

"I get it. I wasn't thinking. I'll take him back." I reached for the dog.

Sabrina looked up at me, those bright blue eyes I loved shining. "I mean..." She hugged him to her.

"I'm heading back to Denver tomorrow," I said abruptly, my mind filling with darkness and self-doubt. "I need to get back."

"You are? Now? Did you just decide this, or...?"

"I've been putting it off."

"Right," she said softly. "Okay, well—"

I stood, not giving her a chance to finish. I reached for the puppy, cradling him to my chest as Sabrina looked up at me, a mixture of disappointment and concern on her face.

"I made soup," I told her. "Help yourself. I'll deal with this guy, and probably turn in early so I can get an early start."

"Ah. Yeah. Okay." She didn't move.

I wanted to take it all back, to undo everything that had just spewed out of my mouth. But it was the right thing to do. I couldn't stay here. This life wasn't my life. And now that Dad was settled and they'd told me not to visit, what was the point of staying? I could sell the shop from a distance.

I went upstairs, taking the puppy outside first and waiting an eternity for him to go to the bathroom. Then I hauled up all the puppy's belongings, tucked him into his crate for the night, and went to bed.

In the morning, I packed my things, and when Sabrina awoke, I was finishing a cup of coffee, my helmet on the table at my side.

"So that's it?" she said. She wore sleep shorts and a long T-shirt, and her hair was in messy spikes around her face. She looked tired. And sad.

"I'll be back for the wedding. I said I would."

She shook her head. "I think it might be better if you don't come back."

I stared at her. "Right." Of course she was right. A clean break. "Okay."

"What will you do with him?" She pointed to the puppy, who was gamboling around at our feet, growling at a stuffed toy I'd gotten for him.

"I think I'm going to take him with me."

"On a motorcycle?"

I nodded and picked up the backpack by my feet. "He can ride in here." There were mesh panels at the top, but the cold wind would probably mean he'd be happier to stay down in the bottom and sleep. "I'll just stop a bit more often."

"Zane."

"Thanks for everything," I told her. "I sent you two months' rent this morning. Check your email."

"You didn't have to."

"That was the agreement. Thanks."

"Should we just shake hands now? Like business associates?" Sabrina laughed, but there was a cutting edge to the question. She was hurt.

I pulled her into a quick hug, my body screaming not to let her go. But I did. And then I tucked the pup into the bag, strapped it onto my chest, picked up my helmet, and walked away.

And with every mile I rode away, more and more of my heart crumbled.

# Chapter Eighteen

## Sabrina

He was gone.

And I was right.

I was a mess.

I told myself not to fall, I told myself I'd be a puddle when it ended. And from the very beginning, I'd known it would end. And my heart was broken over both him and the adorable puppy I just couldn't have.

Besides Zane leaving, the second shop location had problems I hadn't anticipated.

"What do you mean?" I asked the electrician who was shaking his head at his clipboard.

"I don't know who wired these outlets, but if you're going to be running any kind of equipment beyond a fan, we need to get GFCIs in here. And that panel board is overloaded. That's a fire hazard." He made a wide-eyed expression, as if emphasizing how seriously I should be taking this.

I was taking it seriously. So was my wallet. "Can we fix it?"

"Yeah. Just need a week or so."

"How much will this cost?"

The guy quoted a number that made me cringe, but I signed

the work order, and he got started as I sank into a chair in the corner. The world felt less bright and beautiful suddenly, and I just wanted to go back to bed.

"What an ass," Alex said over wine a few days later after I'd told them what happened with Zane.

Anya clinked her glass with Alex's. "Amen to that. Good riddance, right?"

"No, guys." Even my voice was miserable, cracked and husky from crying and then from trying not to cry. "Don't do that. He isn't an ass. He never promised me anything, and he told me right from the start that he'd leave. This is on me."

Alex blew a raspberry in response to that. "I want to be mad at someone," she complained. "I hate seeing you like this. Who can we beat up?"

I tilted my head and gave her tiny form a quick up-and-down look. "You might be able to beat up a blind clawless kitten. Maybe."

"I was speaking figuratively," she said, pulling herself up taller. Alex was at least an inch and a good fifteen pounds smaller than me.

"And I got called 'Squirt,' at Thanksgiving," I said, trying to lighten the mood.

Anya let out a big sigh and gave me a weepy look. "For the record, I hate this. But I also know we need to move on, right?"

"Right," I agreed.

"So. Tell us about the new place." She said this in a gleeful and upbeat voice that made me want to deliver good news, but I couldn't.

"I thought I'd be open right after Thanksgiving, but the place isn't quite as turnkey as I was led to believe."

Alex shook her head. "What?"

"The oven in the back doesn't heat to temperature and there are some electrical code violations that have to be corrected before I'll pass inspection."

Alex and Anya exchanged a look that told me their lawyerly instincts were ramping up.

"I'm not suing anyone, guys."

Anya sighed again.

"So what needs doing? How long?" Alex asked.

"The electrician has already started getting everything fixed. And the new oven won't be in until next Monday. I can open before the oven gets here; I'll just have to bring baked goods from the other location."

"Good plan," Anya said, clearly looking for any news that might be considered vaguely good.

"Yeah..." I deflated. No matter how hard I tried, every other thought pulled me back to Zane, to my silent house, to my aching heart.

"Have you talked to him at all?" Alex asked.

I shook my head. "We agreed on a clean break."

Anya pointed at me. "This is far from clean. You'd need a lobotomy for that."

"Do you think there's some kind of hypnotherapy that could make me forget him? Or just forget that I fell in love with him?" I asked.

Alex put an arm around me and pulled me close. "Oh honey."

We finished up early, and by nine-thirty, I was back in my truck, headed to my quiet house. I took a couple detours on purpose, not eager to find myself alone again in a house where everything reminded me of something—someone—I could not have.

The streets of Holly Creek were quiet, even though it was a Saturday night. But they were bright, with holiday lights strung across every imaginable expanse of space. The central tree glowed so brightly I could see it's shine illuminating the sky from the front yard of my house over a mile away.

I used to love how over the top this town went for the holidays, but now it felt flat. Almost like it was doing exactly what Anya and Alex had been doing—trying too hard to make me happy. To make me forget that I'd given my heart to someone who thought giving me a dog would be an adequate exchange.

Without planning it, I drove slowly by Crosby Metalworks, bringing the car to an idle in front of the two-story building and staring at the "For Sale" sign in the window. There was nothing of Zane here, not really. It wasn't like it was a place we had memories together. But I knew it was where he'd spent most of an unhappy childhood, and some part of me blamed those years for what had happened with us.

Had he assumed it wouldn't work? Had he taken the hurt of his past and projected it onto our future? Or had we had no future from the beginning? Why was I trying to psychoanalyze someone who wasn't even here?

I drove on, heading home and going straight to bed.

# Chapter Nineteen

## Zane

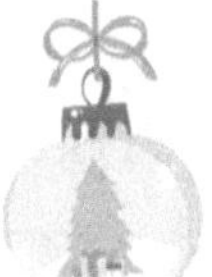

I rode into Denver just after midnight, as snow was beginning to fall. It didn't feel as cold here as it had back home, but Colorado wasn't moist like New York. The city was still awake as I guided my bike through the busy streets, through Aurora and finally down Colfax all the way out toward the River North neighborhood where I'd bought the workshop building a decade ago.

Back then, the neighborhood had been pretty rough. Now it was full of trendy bars and restaurants, and there was no shortage of foot traffic wandering the sidewalks, even with the weather turning.

I would liked to have headed to the loft. But I'd sublet it, and I doubted very much that Rebecca's friend would appreciate me showing up at this late hour with a puppy and demanding a bed. So we went to the metalworks shop instead.

The front of the shop was faced with a metal door next to a roll-down garage-style door, and the back had two roll-downs. It made it nice during the hotter days to work in there, to let the breeze come through from both sides. It also made it easy to find a safe place to stash my bike, since street parking was at a premium, and I'd already learned that leaving it out overnight down here wasn't a good plan.

I pushed the bike up to the front door, ignoring the complaints of the random pedestrians wandering around, and pushed my key into the lock. As I pulled open the familiar door, leaving the bike outside for just a second, I glanced down into the bag on my chest, the little pile of fur inside making my empty heart soften just a bit.

Once the garage door was up and then down, the bike safely inside and the front door locked, I pulled off my helmet and flipped on the lights, and then removed the pack gently and lowered it to the floor.

"Hey, little partner," I crooned as the brown and white pup padded out of the top of the bag, blinking at me sleepily. He glanced around himself, opened his jaws in an enormous yawn, and then took two steps away from the bag and peed all over the shop floor.

It wasn't ideal, but I couldn't help myself. I dropped onto my ass on the floor next to him and laughed. It was partly some form of hysterics, drawn out of me by the endless time on the road, and partly just a need to hear my own voice, to make sure I was still living.

Leaving Sabrina and Dad back in Holly Creek had seemed like the right thing to do. Right up until I crossed the border into Kansas. And then all the way through Kansas and Nebraska, I'd waffled. By the time I entered Colorado, my mind had taken a different tack.

I'd been scared and confused. And hurt. They'd sent me away from Dad, and I'd had no other reason to be in Holly Creek, not really. And as I'd wandered Sabrina's neighborhood, I'd realized that was exactly what it was. Her neighborhood. Her life. I'd told myself I was just attaching myself, that none of it was mine. And in my fucked-up state of mind, I'd decided that giving her the puppy she'd hinted at wanting would somehow seal us together, provide a connection from my lonely island to her full and loving life that I could hang onto.

But it had been the wrong thing.

And so I'd done pretty much the same thing I'd done a decade ago. I'd run away. I'd told myself I didn't need anyone, but every mile away from Sabrina proved it wasn't true.

"Let's get you cleaned up," I told the pup, who followed me in a clumsy prance to the bathroom tucked to one side of the big warehouse space. I grabbed a mess of paper towels and returned to mop up his puddle.

He watched with interest, his dark eyes following my every move. "You're not supposed to pee on the floor," I told him. "But I guess that's better than in the pack."

He dropped his little bottom to the floor and tilted his head at me.

"Yes," I told him, chuckling as I gave his chin a scratch. "You're adorable. It'll get you a long way in life."

When I'd gotten him cleaned up and fed with the last of the kibble I'd brought on the ride, I pulled the cot I stored here out of the storage closet and spread out the sleeping bag. I'd bought these when I'd first moved out here, when I'd slept in the shop regularly as I built the business and looked for a place to live.

The act of setting up that old bed took me back ten years, and I realized with disgust that I'd gotten nowhere in all that time. I was still doing the same things I'd done then, telling myself the same stories. And I was every bit as alone now as I'd been a decade ago.

"Pathetic," I told the dog.

I sat on the edge of the cot, hungry but unwilling to go out looking for food. I stared around the shop. Johnathan had been busy. The enormous fence we'd been working on for months lay in pieces across benches with the finished segments in the cart by the wall. One of my sculptures sat unfinished in the far corner, a woman cast in bronze standing in arabesque, her chin thrust up to the sky and her arms behind her, like she was breaking free of something.

The dog had begun sniffing around the floor, wiggling through spaces and ducking under tables to investigate various smells, and I realized I couldn't just let him wander around all night. But I'd left his crate back at Sabrina's.

"What are we going to do with you?" I asked him.

After a quick wander around the shop, I found a sizable box that I was pretty sure he couldn't climb out of, and I arranged a soft towel in the bottom and dropped in a little Tupperware full of water.

"Just for tonight," I told him.

I shut off the lights, tucked myself in with the box at the foot of my bed, and closed my eyes, letting the sounds of the city outside lull us both to sleep.

I woke to a persistent whine that would have been annoying if it wasn't so cute. The puppy.

Groggy, I rubbed my eyes and checked my phone. Just after six.

"Not much of a sleeper, huh?" I asked the little guy. He was pawing the sides of the box.

I pulled on my jeans and boots, and tugged a T-shirt over my head, and then scooped up the pup and took him out the back door to the alley, where he promptly let out everything he'd been holding in onto a dusting of snow.

Naturally I wasn't prepared in any way to pick up dog poop at six a.m., but I figured it out with some of the plastic bags around the shop. What I really needed to do first thing was get this little guy some food and a proper crate. Maybe a little bed to go in it. But this early? There wasn't anything open.

Instead, we headed for the office, and I opened the files where we kept contracts for work.

Johnathan had kept things straight, and I appreciated him for that. But in my absence, those two commissions were on hold and there wasn't a lot else coming in. It was normal to run into a holiday lull, I knew, and it was also a convenient time to offer John some time off.

He appeared around eight, his eyes going wide as he found me sitting at the desk, a puppy in my lap.

"What the hell? Zane?"

"Hey Johnathan. I'm back."

"With a sidekick. Who's this?" Johnathan strode across the little space and lifted the pup from my lap. "Oh, so cute."

"I don't have a name yet."

"Didn't know you were a dog guy. And this one's gonna be huge, huh?"

I stared at the little pup. "He is?"

"Look at his paws! What breed?"

"No clue. I picked him up on a whim."

"You didn't, uh, see the mom?" he asked, an eyebrow raised.

I shrugged. "I wasn't thinking straight."

"Dude, I'd bet money on Great Dane."

I stared at the puppy. It was tiny. It wasn't a great anything. "Great pain, maybe. He likes to pee in the workshop."

The dog whined in response to this slight.

Johnathan took all this in stride and tucked the puppy under his arm, where the dog seemed perfectly happy. "So, what's the story? How are you? Dad okay?"

I leaned forward, putting my elbows on the desk and rubbing my hands through my hair. "Yeah, I guess. I had to move him into a place. He's got dementia."

"Oh shit. I'm sorry." Johnathan dropped into the chair across from me. "So you gonna move back to New York?"

That got my attention. "What?"

"To be closer?"

I'd thought of it, but not in concrete terms. It had felt wrong to leave, but that had been true a decade ago, too. "I don't know. I'm kind of a mess. I didn't really plan to come back, it just kinda happened."

"You accidentally rode two thousand miles on a whim? With a dog?"

"Yeah."

"What's her name?"

I squinted at him. "I told you, the dog's a boy. And I haven't named him."

"Let's see." Johnathan held the pup up at eye level. "How about, 'bad decision?' or 'heartache?' or what about 'running from love?'"

"Quit it."

"There's clearly a woman at the other end of all this."

"Why do you say that?"

"Because you only make rash decisions when someone's forcing you to feel actual emotions. I've seen it before. Don't forget, I've known you a long time."

I did my best to look intimidating. I was John's boss, after all. But it was pointless. "Sabrina."

"Not a good name for a male dog."

"The woman. Her name is Sabrina. I bought the dog for her."

"But you... and the dog... are here."

"Didn't work out."

He raised an eyebrow at me, his fiery red hair catching a glint from the lights overhead as he shook his head. "I see."

"Tell me where we are with things here."

"Wrapping up. Just have those artsy pieces to do, and we can finish the year. A couple gates and stair rails supposed to be coming in late December to deliver in January."

I nodded. "You want some time off?"

He watched me for a long minute. "Yeah, but you going to be okay here?"

"I'll be good."

He shrugged and turned his attention to the dog. "Brutus? No. Leggy?"

"Don't name my dog."

"Someone has to."

"I'll get around to it. I need to see what kind of personality he has first."

"Fair enough. Anything you need before I take off then?" Johnathan stood and handed the pup back to me over the desk.

"Ah, yeah. Actually, could you grab some dog supplies while I figure out what needs doing here? Food, a crate, some bowls?" The puppy had begun chewing on my fingers with its pointy little teeth. "Something to chew on?"

"Sure thing. You gonna take him to the vet? Get him checked out?"

"Yeah. I'll get there."

"Okay, be right back." Johnathan headed out, and I stared at the dog.

"Don't be a Great Dane, okay? That will make it really hard to ride around with you."

The puppy stared at me, and then dropped his head to gnaw on my fingers again.

"Let's find breakfast," I told him. A few minutes later, I'd snapped on the leash I'd brought with us and we were walking down the sidewalk toward the little burrito shop I knew on the corner.

# Chapter Twenty

## Sabrina

The next week was spent driving back and forth between Brewed Awakening locations, setting up the new place as much as I possibly could ahead of the grand opening, which I'd scheduled for December 15th.

The electrician had been through the whole place, and the ceiling was a disaster because he'd cut multiple holes in the plaster and then "patched them." Evidently it was standard for electricians to make holes but not fix them, and now I needed a plasterer to come and smooth out the little squares and circles that were all over the shop's ceiling and apply another coat of paint. At least the electrical was all working now, and was up to code, according to the inspector.

I was given a provisional approval, which would be official once the oven was in and checked out, which meant I could open but I couldn't cook anything besides coffee until that happened.

That was enough.

Now it was down to decor, and Alex and Anya helped a ton with that, dragging me to yard sales and thrift shops to find the perfect eclectic chairs and couches to make the space homey and warm. We picked out tables and lamps, and I found a row of incredible barstools with wrought iron legs that made me think of Zane's work.

Over the course of the cold winter days, my heart didn't heal. But it did seem to be holding together. I went to bed cold and lonely every night, listening to winter's howling winds wrapping my little empty house, and I tried not to think about Zane.

"Oh honey," Chelsea said on the phone when I spoke to her two days before my grand opening. "I wish I could get down there for it, but momzilla has a list as long as my arm of things that need attention before the wedding."

"I understand," I told her, picking up on the notes of happiness and excitement in her voice beyond the irritation with her mother-in-law to be. "Focus on wedding stuff. It's so soon! Are you excited?"

"I am," she said, but I could hear the hesitation in her voice. "It's just all... a lot, you know?"

"A lot of what?"

"I mean... it's at the Plaza, Sabs. And it's like, money is no object for Rex's family. It's crazy."

"Sounds like it's gonna be a good party then. I can't wait." I coaxed some brightness into my voice. I was happy for my friend, and I could celebrate her love even if my own chances of love had dissolved in winter's chill.

"It should be. I'm just... I'm nervous, I guess."

Chelsea didn't come from money, not the way Rex did. I didn't blame her. "We'll be there for you. Remember that this is your wedding, not hers. And it's about you and the amazing guy you fell in love with. Nothing else."

"Thanks for that," she actually sounded more relaxed. "I needed to hear it. You're right."

"Always."

"Hey, good luck with everything. I'm so proud of you, Sabby."

"Thanks."

"See you soon!"

"Bye, Chels." I dropped the phone onto my bedside table and let out a pitiful sigh.

These were the moments when I wondered if I should have let Zane leave that adorable puppy. It was an impulsive gift, that was for sure. And the last thing I needed was that kind of responsibility, considering lately I'd been eating muffins for breakfast and lunch and ramen for dinner if I even bothered. With wine. Lots of wine.

But it might be nice to have some company, and the puppy had been so adorable, brown and white with dark little eyes and a pink nose. I had no idea what kind of dog it was, but I imagined having it snuggled close to me now, and wished I hadn't let it go.

I wished I hadn't let either of them go.

But there was no point thinking about it now. Two more days until the shop opened. I needed to focus.

# Chapter Twenty-One

## Zane

og and I lived at the shop for a few days, and I thought the entire time about what I needed to do.

We couldn't stay here. For one thing, the place wasn't zoned residential, and as soon as someone picked up on the fact I was living here, I'd get a fine. Beyond that? My heart just wasn't in it anymore.

I finished up the final commissions before the new year, and looked around the quiet space.

"What do you think, pup?" I asked the dog, who titled his head and regarded me with curiosity.

I'd never been the kind of guy to follow my heart. Or maybe I'd just never been the kind of guy whose heart told him what to do.

But now? My heart was overpowering every rational thought I had.

"Ready to get back home?" I asked the dog, closing up the shop for the last time. The dog licked me as he looked up from the open top of my bag. I laughed and pulled on my helmet. "Me too."

# Chapter Twenty-Two

## Sabrina

"You ready?" Trent asked me as we stood together behind the counter in the new location of Brewed Awakening on the morning of the opening.

"Nope," I told him. I kept my voice steady, but inside, I was a giddy disaster. We were ready, actually. Everything was shined and polished, the fancy new coffee machine was in top form, cups and merch were all stocked and ready to go... We were still waiting on the oven, but it wasn't going to delay the opening.

Trent smiled at me and squeezed my shoulder. "It's gonna be great."

In the weeks since he'd joined the team as my manager, he'd become so much more than that. I had a great dad, but Trent was becoming kind of a father figure, someone to stand in since Dad was a couple hours away.

I hadn't realized how much I'd come to rely on his wise, calm counsel when things were crazy, but I noticed it when Trent wasn't around now. He made everything run much more smoothly, and even Paul seemed less touchy in general when Trent was around.

"I'll be at the other shop until noon," he said. "And then I promised the wife lunch."

"Is she regretting pushing you out of the house?"

He gave me a wry smile. "She just might be. I think I'm busier now than I was before I retired."

"You don't have to work so hard here," I said, a little worried. I didn't want to overwork him. He might quit and now I couldn't do without him. "Once the shop is open—"

"Sabrina, it's fine. It's like I've got a new lease on life."

"You sure?"

"It's good for the wife too. When I get home, I've got things to talk about. It's much better than just playing golf all the time. She gets tired of listening to me talk about that."

I sighed, feeling gratitude bloom inside me for my friends and coworkers. I lived a very blessed life. "Okay, when it gets to be too much—"

"I'll let you know." His blue eyes twinkled merrily. "I'll be here by two, okay? That'll give us plenty of time for last minute details before we open those doors at four."

The other shop was closing for the afternoon and evening, and we'd had signs up for weeks about the grand opening here. Trent and Paul and I would all be working, and we'd planned a little champagne reception for any of the regulars who wanted to pop in to celebrate.

"See you then, Trent. Thanks for everything."

After he left, I looked around the shop. There was really nothing left to do. We were ready. I decided to go home for a bit, put on the dress I planned to wear for the opening and spend a little extra time on my hair and makeup.

I drove the little truck back to Holly Creek, slowing as I drove past Crosby Metalworks, as had become my humiliating habit. But today, something was different. The little sign I'd come to accept announcing the business as "for sale" was gone.

Now, there was a new sign. It was bigger, brighter. It read, "Under New Management."

My heart sank.

That was it, then. Zane had sold the shop and he was gone for good. I was sure he'd pop into town to visit his dad... wouldn't he? But at this point I wasn't at all certain I'd be any part of those visits. What would be the point?

He had texted me once, actually. But the words didn't offer any hope for a future for us, no matter how many times I pulled out my phone to reread them, which I did again as I pulled into my driveway.

Zane: Good luck tonight. The new shop will be great.

It was friendly. Polite.

And that was all I should expect at this point, even if my heart stuttered in frustration at the thought.

A few hours later, wearing a bright pink A-line dress and heels that I'd chosen to contrast my freshly tinted blue-tipped locks, I pulled into the little parking lot behind the new location.

I unlocked the back door and went in, seeing it in its pre-open state for the last time. Despite my lingering sadness, I took deep breaths and focused myself on gratitude. This was the achievement I'd been working for, and I'd finally done it. With the new shop, and with Trent and Paul by my side to help run things, I was on the brink of the next phase of my life.

Once things were up and running smoothly, I planned to take some time off. I wanted to travel a little bit, see something besides the walls of my own business. And the extra income I hoped this commuter-heavy location would bring in should be enough to make it happen.

I walked through the space and felt my soul lighten. I'd done this. And no matter what else wasn't exactly right in my life, I could handle that too.

By the time Trent and I were flipping the sign and pushing open the glass doors out front, I felt gleeful. This was it.

"Thirty-seven large caramel macchiatos, please!" Alex cried, practically sprinting through the doors to give me a hug.

"Oh god, no," I moaned. "I hope no one shows up tonight with an order like that!"

Anya walked in behind her, carrying Charlie, who refrained from calling me Squirt. I'd take small blessings where they came.

I handed my friends some champagne as more guests trickled in, a combination of regulars from the other location and new customers. By the time Peter and Charlotte arrived, there wasn't a seat to be found. Trent spotted pregnant Charlotte right away, however, and magically produced a stool that had been in the back.

"You made it!" I hugged them both, feeling giddy.

"Of course, sis. This is a big deal. You're a coffee mogul now." Peter gave me a grin laced with something I knew was pride.

"There she is," another voice boomed from the door, and I turned in shock as my father came in, my mom at his side.

"I didn't know you guys were coming," I felt tears pressing behind my eyes. Maybe that second glass of champagne had been a bad idea.

"Wouldn't miss it, baby," Mom said, kissing my cheek and giving me a warm hug.

"How was the cruise?" I asked. She and Dad gave me a brief summary of their latest trip and then toasted my new shop with me before sending me into the crowd to mingle while they chatted with Charlotte and Peter.

The music was low, but I'd selected a list of holiday classics and cheery tunes, and between the lights we'd strung inside and the happy chatter of my friends, family, and guests, the shop had turned into a whole other world. It was a world that held absolutely everything and everyone that mattered to me. Except my other brothers and sisters, who were scattered around the world... and Zane.

For two hours, I flitted from group to group, chatting with friends and new faces, and finally, I took a break and closed myself in the bathroom, which I'd painted a Tiffany blue. I stared into the mirror and took a few deep steadying breaths when I'd finished washing my hands, and the woman I saw there made me proud.

When I stepped back out into the madness, feeling refreshed, I knew immediately that something was different. There was a shift in the hum of conversation, a subtle change in the atmosphere.

Paul stepped close to my side and murmured in my ear. "I'll tell him to get lost if you want."

I frowned up at him and then scanned the crowd again, my eyes snagging on a familiar head of black hair near the door. Zane?

"It's okay," I breathed, sure I must be seeing things.

I moved through the crowd to where he stood, looking around uncertainly. He wore a red plaid button-down shirt and black slacks. I didn't think I'd ever seen him out of a T-shirt and jeans, and the look was devastating to my already wounded heart.

He spotted me, and the dark eyes widened, sending sparks flying inside my chest. His sexy smirk shifted into a full-on smile, and I wanted to run to him.

But I couldn't. We'd already closed that door.

"Hi," I said, stepping as close as I dared.

"Congratulations, Sabrina. This is amazing. Look at all these people."

I glanced around, having practically forgotten what was going on. A few eyes watched us with interest, and Paul and my brother both looked ready to throw down at a moment's notice.

"Yeah, thanks. Um, what are you doing here?"

I couldn't look him directly in the eyes while I waited for him to answer, there was too much turmoil inside me, and meeting his eyes just made me long for everything I'd been silly enough to think we could have.

"I came for you," he said quietly, and I was sure I'd misheard him.

"You came all this way for a coffee shop opening?"

"No, Sabrina." Zane took my hand, snapping my attention to him, forcing me to meet that smoky gaze that had me wanting to fling myself at him. "I came back for you." Zane looked around, as if noticing the crowd and the festive atmosphere for the first time. "I wanted to be here because the shop opening is important, but I came back to Holly Creek because I'm in love with you, and I didn't like being away."

I stared at him.

The words were simple and clear, and my heart understood them perfectly. But my mind refused to make sense of the message he'd just delivered.

"You're..."

Zane still held my hand, and now he gave it a tiny tug, bringing me a step closer to his broad chest. His other hand lifted to trace a line down my cheek, and the look in his eyes as he did it was so purely loving, I nearly sank to my knees. "I'm in love with you," he said again. "And I'm staying in Holly Creek."

I blinked hard to make sure I was actually awake because I was pretty sure I'd had this dream once before. But when my vision cleared, Zane was still before me, my hand in his and his other hand resting on my shoulder.

"Now you're making me nervous," he said.

I was having a lot of trouble finding words. "Oh, um..."

Zane looked around again, a hint of distress erasing the calm expression he'd worn when he'd told me... Told me that he... loved me. "I can go," he said, taking a step backward. "Maybe we can talk later?"

"No," I said, tightening my grasp on his hand. My mouth wasn't working properly but the rest of my body seemed willing to put up a fight for what I wanted. "No, stay."

"Okay."

"And we'll talk later?"

Zane stepped close and dropped a soft kiss on my forehead. "I'll be right here." And then he let me go, and I turned and walked to the back of the shop, passing through the crowd without seeing anyone and finding a quiet spot in the kitchen where I could try to take stock.

"Sabs?" Anya followed me in.

I turned and stared at her. "Zane is here."

"I saw that. And I saw him hold your hand and kiss you and say words to you."

"He did. He said words."

She crossed her arms and gave me an evaluative look. "Men don't cross countries to finish breaking up with people or remind people they broke up with that they're well and truly done. Do they?"

"I don't think so."

Anya stepped closer and peered into my face. My brain fog was beginning to lift and actual processing was happening in there now.

"He said he came back for me."

"Aha, that explains why you're hiding in here."

I shook my head, sending the remaining fog scattering. "I'm just confused."

"What's confusing?"

"He said he loves me."

Anya let out a high-pitched squeal that was very atypical of her. "Ohmygod!" she cried. "That's amazing!"

"Yeah." It was, it was just so very unexpected.

"You're happy, right?"

I nodded. "Of course." What was wrong with me then? "I guess... I guess it just might not change anything. I mean, Anya, he lives in Denver. He sold the business here. He said he's staying here, but he lives there."

"Right. So what's the plan?"

"I don't know. I was having trouble forming actual words, so it wasn't much of an in-depth examination of what the future might hold for us."

"Do you love him?" she asked.

Did I? I searched around inside myself, looking for something bright and glowing that might be labeled "love for Zane." But what I found instead were echoes of feelings. The way I got all melty and warm when he smiled at me. The way my overprotective instincts kicked in when I thought about him being judged or bullied as a kid. The way I wanted to go back in time and rescue teenaged Zane so he didn't have to spend a second thinking he wasn't loved or wanted.

Because he was.

I loved Zane. I wanted him.

"Yeah. I love Zane."

"Then you'll make it work," she promised me. I looked into my friend's sparkling blue eyes and felt my heart lift with hope. I believed her. I was afraid my heart wouldn't survive if he left again. But he'd said he was staying, and I had to take the chance.

"What do I do now?" I asked her as she pulled me into a tight hug.

"Let's finish up this event and get everyone gone so you guys can be alone!"

I looked at the clock. It was after eight. I planned to shut everything down at nine, so there wasn't long to wait.

Anya and I went back out, and for the next hour, I did my best to chat and serve food and drinks, but part of me was near the door, sitting with Zane. He was waiting patiently, a glass of water in his hand, and his eyes found mine repeatedly, sending little jolts of expectation through me.

Alex and Charlie had left hours ago, and my mother and father had departed soon after they did. Peter and Charlotte came to say goodbye just before the crowd began to trickle out rapidly. By nine, I was saying goodbye to Anya, who whispered something to Zane that sounded suspiciously like, "hurt her again and you die."

Trent and Paul stood shoulder to shoulder as I returned from wishing the last customer well and got ready to clean up.

"You go," Paul said.

"We've got this," Trent agreed, and then his eyes moved to where Zane sat patiently waiting for me.

"But only if that's what you want," Paul said. "Offer still stands. I'll throw his ass out in the snow."

I laughed, part nerves and part love for my loyal friend. "That's not necessary." I glanced back at Zane and made up my mind. "If you guys don't mind, I'd love if you'd close up. Thank you for everything tonight. This was amazing and I couldn't have done it without you both. You're the best."

I found myself in an awkward group hug then, and happiness surged through me. No matter what happened with Zane, I had this.

"Now go," Trent said, giving me a fatherly smile.

I gathered my bag and retrieved my coat, and then I walked to stand in front of Zane. He rose without a word, pulled on his own coat, and we stepped out into the snowy December night together.

# Chapter Twenty-Three

## Zane

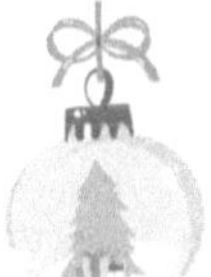

"Um..." Sabrina said, and I could feel the tension wafting off her. There was so much to tell her, so much to explain. But a freezing cold sidewalk wasn't the place.

"Did you ride your bike here?" she asked.

"I Ubered, actually," I told her.

"Do you need a ride, then?"

"Sure, but how about I drive? You've had a long night."

"Okay." She handed me the keys and I got her settled in the little cab of the truck, coming around the side to find her poking at the buttons to get the heat going.

"Do you need a place to stay?" she asked.

"Did you rent out my room yet?"

"Not yet." She sounded uncertain, and I didn't blame her.

"I actually have my own place," I told her, glancing to see her expression as I guided the truck toward Holly Creek. "Want to come see it?"

She was staring at me now, her mouth slightly open and those eyes sharp and assessing, glinting in the low light coming from the radio console. "Okay," she said.

"I got back yesterday," I told her. "But I wanted to get some things settled and I knew your big opening was tonight. Maybe it wasn't the right thing to just appear..."

"You were here yesterday?" she asked.

I shot her a quick look. Was she upset? She still hadn't really commented on the fact I'd told her I was in love with her. Those were words I'd actually never said to anyone, and to have them hanging out there, potentially unrequited, was slowly eating away at the confidence I'd felt all day yesterday as I got things ready for this moment.

"Yeah, sorry. I just wanted everything to be done. To be sure about stuff."

"What stuff?"

"I'm moving back for good, Sabrina. To be closer to Dad. To be with you, if you'll have me."

She sniffed, and I glanced at her again, still terrified she'd say no.

"Zane," she said softly, and then she made a sound that had me ready to pull the truck over. Was she crying? But no, then it sounded like laughter. She was smiling, but there were tears running down her cheeks.

"Yeah?"

"I just... I think I'm in shock."

"Good shock?"

"Is that a thing?"

I blew out a breath. "Sabrina, I'm dying over here. Are you happy to see me?"

"So happy. But I still feel like maybe I just hoped so much that you'd come back that I manifested a super realistic hallucination or something. What about your shop? Your life in Denver?"

"None of it was anything I couldn't move. And the people I love are here. It didn't make sense to stay there."

We drove in silence for a while, and as much as I wanted to

give Sabrina the time she needed to adjust, I was on the edge of my seat. I still wasn't sure what she was thinking.

"Are we going to your dad's shop?" she asked, breaking the long silence when I turned into downtown Holly Creek.

"Yeah. My shop now. And my apartment. I bought the building and the business."

Sabrina didn't say anything, but I saw her sit up straighter, as if this news physically impacted her.

I parked her truck around the back in front of the garage that held my motorcycle and the truck I'd just bought.

And then, with my heart in my throat, I went around and helped Sabrina out of the car and up the back stairs to my new —and old—apartment.

With all of Dad's stuff gone, it had been easy enough to clean and have painted from Denver, and some of the furniture I'd ordered had come in, while I'd grabbed a few other things in the truck the day before.

"Welcome," I told her as I unlocked the door and waved her inside. I flipped on the overhead light in the living room, and Sabrina looked around, and then let out a little gulp when she spotted the crate against the far wall.

Someone else was making a fair amount of noise too. It was the longest I'd left the puppy on his own so far, and I hoped he was okay.

"You kept him?"

"Yeah... I think he helped me realize what I really wanted." I let the pup out of his crate, and he bolted straight at Sabrina, not quite stopping before crashing into her legs. He was already bigger than the last time she'd seen him, and he looked like a different dog.

"He's huge," she laughed, bending down to pet his increasingly massive head.

"I think he might be a Great Dane."

"Oh my god." Sabrina laughed, and the sound filled my heart.

I wanted to hear that laugh for the rest of my life. "What did you name him?"

"I haven't yet. I'm waiting for the right thing."

She shot me a look then, her mouth dropping into a little disappointed 'o.' "You have to give him a name!"

"I will. Maybe you can help. First, he probably needs to go out for a minute. Will you wait?"

"Of course," she said, looking around the living room as she stood.

"Make yourself at home," I told her, attaching the leash to the dog's collar and hoping she would do exactly that. I thought I'd be happiest if she never, ever left.

Once the dog had finished up outside, we headed back in, and I joined Sabrina where she sat on the long grey leather couch.

"This place is gorgeous, Zane."

"Thanks."

"Is it hard being here? Where you and your dad lived?"

I knew she was referring to my less-than-ideal childhood. "In a way it feels like the right thing. Like I'm chasing out the old ghosts, you know?"

She nodded. There was a silent beat and then quietly, "I missed you."

I turned my body to face her, wanting so much to touch her, to hold her. "I missed you too."

"I'm sorry it's taken me a little while to process what you said to me at the shop," she began. "I just... it was so unexpected."

I wanted to interrupt to tell her again how much I loved her, but I had the sense she was about to say something else.

Her bright blue eyes met mine, and for a second, the world stopped moving. Even the dog dropped to his haunches and stared up at her.

"The thing is, Zane," she began, her voice soft and uncertain. "I love you too. But it's terrifying to say that to you. You left...

You basically ran away. And I guess I'm just afraid that if I trust you. If I love you... It's handing you the power to hurt me again."

She loved me. That was all I needed. I reached for her hand, and she gave it to me, turning to face me on the couch, her legs tucked under her.

"I'm so sorry I hurt you," I told her. "You scared the shit out of me."

She let out a laugh. "I scared you?"

"Yeah. You're so open and free with your emotions and your love. And I just... I've kept myself guarded. It's easier. Less chance of getting hurt. And when I realized I was in love with you, I guess part of me thought that getting away from you would fix it. That if I could just not be in love with you, then I could protect myself. But it didn't work."

The dog was busily sniffing around now, but then he settled, happily chewing on the leg of a brand new dining chair. "Hey!" I snapped at him. He stopped for a second, gave me a "what you gonna do about it?" look and then resumed. Dog training would have to happen soon.

Sabrina was smiling, and when I met her eyes, my heart seized. "I love you too, Zane. And I'm so glad you're back. I can't believe you're moving here!"

"Moved," I corrected.

"I can't believe you live here!" she threw herself at me, and as her arms went around my neck, my world snapped itself back together. This. This was all I needed.

I pulled her close to me, breathing her in, feeling her exactly where she belonged. That hug went on for long, long minutes. Or maybe hours or centuries. But soon, Sabrina's soft fingers began tracing lines along my jaw, her eyes meeting mine. And when the tension between us had absorbed as much happy anticipation as it could hold, I pressed my lips to hers, unleashing every ounce of desire I had for her in a single kiss.

"Show me the bedroom please," she murmured, pulling her

mouth from mine as her fingers worked down the buttons on my shirt.

"Right this way," I said, scooping her off the couch and carrying her into the bedroom where my king-sized bed had just been set up.

I set her on the end of the fluffy dark teal duvet and let myself look at her for a long moment. "You're so beautiful," I told her. And then I took my time, removing her dress carefully and draping it over a chair before kicking free of my shoes and my pants. She stood and helped me out of the shirt I was still wearing, and my hands explored the wonders of her soft curvy body, reveling in the slide of soft skin, the breathy moans she released when I cupped her breast over the sheer lace of her bra.

"Come here." I took her hand and walked her around to the head of the bed, pulling down the comforter with my other hand and then helping her in. I'd had the heat fixed in the shop, but it was still chilly, and sliding into the warmth of the thick sheets and blankets was welcome.

We slid together, our bodies locked as if we were afraid to let go, and we kissed and explored one another until the space around us in the bed warmed up. Then I moved Sabrina so she was lying on top of me, every inch of her body pressed to mine.

"God, I missed you."

"I missed you too," she said, sitting up to straddle me. She reached behind her and a second later, her bra slid from her arms and my hands moved to hold her breasts.

"So perfect," I told her, caressing her and then letting my thumbs slide over the taut nipples as she took in a sharp breath.

She was moving over me, rubbing her center against the hard length of my cock, and it was building the need inside me, but I didn't want to rush things. She was in control, and I could hold out forever if it meant being with Sabrina.

A long low groan escaped her lips as she moved, and it ratcheted up my desire. I found her ass and guided her over me again, loving the friction and the way she moaned as her clit found the stimulation it needed.

She shifted and peeled off her panties, climbing off of me long enough for me to pull off my boxer briefs, and then she was back, her hot flesh sliding along mine until I thought I would burst.

"Condom?" she breathed.

I pointed to the bedside table, and she leaned over just enough to drop one perfect breast into my mouth. I sucked and teased, and she collapsed onto me for a moment, crying out, before remembering her mission.

A moment later, she was rolling the length down me, and then meeting my eyes as she notched me at her entrance. She didn't break eye contact as she slid lower, more slowly than I thought I could take. That connection between us was so complete I could have finished right then, more from the eye contact than from the way her slick channel was eating up my aching cock—though that was devastating in its own right.

When she began to move, slowly rising up and then crashing back down on me, I was lost.

Luckily, she didn't need long. I dropped a hand between us, adding friction where she needed it, and she began to moan with every thrust.

"Oh."

"Oh."

"Ohhhhh."

"Oh god."

"Ohhhhh Zaaaaaane."

I wasn't going to last much longer. I felt a pulse from her as she took me all the way in again, and then it was like she finally let go, and I felt the fluttering pull of her orgasm against me as she cried out.

I thrust upward once, twice, and then my body uncoiled. It was perfect. Everything about her, about us, was perfect.

And when she collapsed against me, I held her until our breathing slowed, and all I heard was a low questioning whine.

"Is that you?" she asked me.

"No. I thought it was you."

We turned our heads at the same time to find the puppy staring up at us from the side of the bed, his big head tilted to one side.

"Get used to it," I told him.

Sabrina laughed.

# Chapter Twenty-Four

## Zane

Settling back into Holly Creek was surprisingly easy.

But this time, everything was different.

I had a home. I was running a business. And there was Sabrina. And Dog. I had a life.

Winter had set in for real, but the people of this crazy little town embraced the snow and ice with gusto, amping up their holiday cheer with every step we took closer to Christmas.

Sabrina and I spent a lot of time going and back and forth from her house to my house, Dog in tow. She'd kept the items I'd bought for him when I'd first picked him up and given him to her, but the crate I'd bought then was already becoming a tight squeeze.

"We can't go on like this," Sabrina told me one night, a week before our trip to NYC for her friend Chelsea's wedding.

A spike of worry sliced through me and I sat up straighter, her feet still in my lap and Dog still wedged between us on the couch at her house.

"We can't?" I said, working to keep my voice steady. Our stability was still new, and there was a part of me that expected it to come crashing down. I was too happy. Things were too good.

She shook her head, but made no move to get up. The movie continued playing in front of us and she wiggled her toes in silent encouragement to keep rubbing her feet. "No. This dog needs a real name. It's hard enough trying to train him, especially when we don't have a name he associates with himself."

I raised an eyebrow at her. So far, Dog had not proven himself to be a rocket scientist. "I'm not sure that matters."

She blew out a breath in mock frustration. "How many dogs have you trained, Zane?"

I thought about that, taking a long, drawn-out moment to look up at the ceiling while I counted in my head. "None." I pointed at her. "Your number?"

"Well, none."

"Ha!"

"But how many dog training books have you read?" she asked me now. Dog climbed over to her lap and pushed his head against her chest, like he was taking her side.

"Also none."

"Right. And I've read at least four since this lug came to live with us. We need to give him a name. Pronto."

"You want to call him Pronto?" I was half-joking.

"It's not bad..." she shook her head. "No. That's not it."

"How about Rudy, since he's a Christmas dog?"

"For Rudolph? I like it... but no."

We didn't decide on anything that night. And over the following days, we'd throw ideas at each other, poor Dog snapping his head back and forth as we considered each option.

"Hugo?" Sabrina asked as she picked up her bag to head to work.

"No. Rally?" I suggested, picking up my own stuff and gathering a few of Dog's toys to take to the shop where he hung out while I worked.

"Nope."

A day later, Alex and Anya were over with Charlie, and the babies—dog and boy—tussled on the floor while we sat on the couch watching.

"How about something standard?" Anya asked. "Rex or Spot?"

"Boring!" Sabrina cried. "We need something meaningful, interesting."

"Definitely," Alex agreed. "How about 'Love Reclaimed'?"

I threw a pillow at her.

"That sounds like a cheesy romance novel," Anya said. "Or a good one, maybe."

I sighed, ready to give up and just call him Dog forever, when Charlie jumped to his feet and stepped near to his Aunt Sabrina's side. "Squirt!" he cried, only this time, he wasn't looking at Sabrina, he was looking at Dog.

"I've about had it with that nickname, Charlie," Sabrina told him, but her face was lit up in an amused smile.

Charlie pointed at Dog. "No. You're Auntie Sab. He is Squirt."

We all stared at Dog, as if letting the name settle onto him to see if it fit right.

"Squirt?" I said, trying it out. "Kind of ironic. He's going to be huge."

"I like it," Anya said.

"Squirt," Sabrina repeated. "Yep. It fits. And if he's Squirt, then no one gets to call me that anymore, right, Charlie?"

Charlie laughed and a huge grin spread across his face. "I named the dog."

"You did," I agreed. "Good job. We couldn't seem to do it."

The next day, we went to pick up Dad. Holly Hills had called every other day to report how he was adjusting, and each call was full of surprises. Dad was playing checkers with the men who gathered each evening in the common area. Dad was having dinner with some lady friends he'd met in the garden. Dad was joining an exercise class?

I hadn't seen him since I'd left him there, and my heart was uncomfortable in my chest as I parked the extra cab truck at the curb out front.

"You ready?" Sabrina asked.

"I don't know. I still feel really guilty. What if he's angry at me for leaving him?"

"It doesn't sound like it so far," she said, reminding me of the calls I'd gotten.

"You coming in?"

"I'll stay with Squirt and let you say hello," she said, snapping the dog's leash to his collar and pointing out at the big open lawn next to the parking lot that had some patches of brown grass showing through the snow.

"Okay."

I went in, signed the paperwork they gave me and then followed the concierge down the hall to the common room, where she said Dad usually hung out in the mornings.

We stepped into a bright airy space filled with comfortable furniture and tables that were populated with a variety of people involved in various pursuits. A group of women filled one couch, walkers and canes pushed to the side as they held coffee cups and talked in quiet voices. At another table, some men were involved in what looked like a game of poker. There were a few people scattered on their own near windows, reading or just sitting.

And then there was Dad. He was sitting with three women at a table, holding a hand of cards in front of him.

"He's been learning to play bridge," the concierge told me.

"Isn't that a pretty complicated game?" I asked. The last time I'd seen Dad play cards, he was struggling with Go Fish.

"It is," she said, and then she inclined her head and whispered, "they're not a very discerning crowd. Not really sticklers for the rules."

I watched for a moment, smiling at the thought of them sort of playing bridge and no one caring if it was right or not.

As if feeling the weight of my eyes on him, Dad lifted his head and looked around. Tension gripped my stomach as I waited for him to spot me. Would he even know who I was?

Dad's eyes found my face, and there was no pause before his face broke into a wide, happy grin. I heard him say to the ladies at the table, "Excuse me, girls. That's my boy over there. We're having lunch." And as all three ladies turned to watch, he rose and crossed the room on shaky legs to step close. His arm was out of the huge cast, but he still wore a sling, and he clapped me on the back with his other hand, the smile never fading. "Good to see you, Son."

"Hi Dad," I said, giving his shoulders a little squeeze.

My heart had leapt into my throat and seemed to be stuck there, making me feel alternately sick and like I might actually cry. Dad seemed happy, settled. Better than I'd ever seen him looking, actually.

"How are you doing?" I asked, ready for him to unleash his anger at being moved here against his will.

"I'm great," he said. "It's like living at a resort all the time." He leaned close. "And there are a lot of single women here." He wiggled his eyebrows at me as surprise trickled through my body. Dad was on the hunt?

"Well, good," I said, unsure how to respond to this version of Dad. "Are you still up for going out to lunch with me and Sabrina?"

"The girlfriend," he said, part question, part statement.

"Right. My girlfriend. And we brought Squirt, our dog."

Dad made a face at that. I had no idea if he liked animals - we'd never had pets when I was a kid.

"Okay, let's go," he said, steeling his face like meeting this dog was akin to marching off to the front as he pulled on his coat.

Out front, Sabrina and Squirt spotted us and came over to say hi to Dad.

"Mr. Crosby," Sabrina said. "It's so nice to see you again."

"Dad, you remember Sabrina."

"A pleasure," Dad said. And then he bent down and offered his hand to Squirt who sniffed it and then immediately pressed his entire body against Dad's legs.

"You're in!" Sabrina laughed.

We climbed into the truck, which had an extended cab, and Sabrina settled in the back seat with Squirt. We took Dad to a cafe that had a heated outdoor patio that allowed dogs, and I became more and more relaxed as the day wore on.

Sabrina was great with him, engaging him in conversation about everything from his hobbies at Holly Hills to the wedding we were traveling to attend the following weekend.

"That's great," Dad said, his eyes watery suddenly. "I just wish I could come."

Sabrina and exchanged a look.

"You want to go to New York?" I asked him.

"To see my son get married? Yes," he said. "But I'm not sure I can do it."

A laugh escaped my chest, and I shook my head. "No, Dad. Sabrina and I aren't getting married." My eyes found hers. "Yet."

Sabrina's eyes glowed and she held my gaze for a long moment, and then she returned her eyes to my father. "It's my best friend's wedding. When Zane and I get married," she glanced at me, "you'll be there for sure."

Dad smiled broadly at that. "Good. And Squirt should come too." Dad and the dog had bonded. Since meeting, Squirt had shown his clear preference for Dad's company by sitting at his side and laying across his feet constantly.

"We'll see," I laughed.

That night, after we'd taken Dad home and Squirt was curled in a sizable ball on his dog bed next to the couch at Sabrina's, she was nestled into my side.

"How are you doing?" she asked me, one of her hands stroking absently across my chest in a way that made it hard to focus on anything else.

"Honestly?" I looked down at her, tugging her a little closer to my side. "I don't think I've ever been happier."

She sighed and dropped her head back against my shoulder. "Me either."

I wanted to ask her something, but wasn't sure how to bring it up. Everything was perfect and there was no part of me that wanted to risk ruining things. Only... I wanted to ask.

"Hey," I started, pulling away a little so I could see her face. "Today with my dad..."

"Yeah?" Those bright blue eyes met mine again. Startling. Every time.

"That thing he said about us getting married."

Sabrina chuckled. "Yeah," she said, and there was a note in her voice that told me she thought I was just bringing up an amusing memory.

"No pressure at all on that."

"Of course not," she laughed.

"But you should know, I wasn't joking."

Her smile crept slowly bigger. "Okay."

"Is that okay with you?"

"Are you asking me if I will allow you to ask me to marry you someday?"

When she put it like that it sounded silly. "I guess so, yeah."

"Hmm." She sat up, tilting her head to one side. "I don't know the protocol for this one. Is this a one-knee question?"

"If you want it to be, it can be." I slid off the couch and got to one knee in front of where she sat, taking one of her hands in mine.

Sabrina began giggling. "I was kidding!"

"I'm not," I said, making myself hold onto my stern expression. "Sabrina," I began, and she quieted down, those big earnest eyes widening. "Will you give me the honor of your permission to ask for the honor of marrying you at some undetermined date in the future?"

She was serious now, and she wrapped her other hand around mine. "Yes," she breathed. "One hundred percent, yes. You have my permission."

The world at that moment was a tightly shimmering ball, a universe contained wholly in the living room of our little house, our big-little dog slumbering noisily nearby. It was a world big enough for only the three of us—my family—and the feeling of everything within it being absolutely everything I'd ever need was overwhelming.

"I love you," I told Sabrina.

"I love you too, Zane," she said. And then she stood, tugging me up by the hand until we were standing, chest to chest. "So much."

And then the world tucked in even tighter around us as I took her face gently in my hand and touched her nose with mine, inhaling the beauty and perfection of the happiest moment I'd ever known, just before I kissed her.

# Epilogue - The Wedding

## Sabrina

The Plaza Hotel was like no place I'd ever stayed in my life. The fact that our room faced Central Park, giving us a view that could have been in a movie scene, was just icing on the cake.

The rehearsal dinner the night before had been an event, to be sure. It was clear Rex's family was pulling out all the stops, but Chelsea had looked so happy, nothing else really mattered. I'd attended the rehearsal, met Zane back in the room for a bit longer than intended, and then we'd dashed into the rehearsal dinner in the Oak Room. Mrs. Buchanan had given me a stern look as we'd come in fifteen minutes late. But Chelsea had just smiled and given me a knowing wink.

Zane and I slipped out early too. The room was just too tempting, and I still wasn't used to having him completely to myself with no distractions from work. Or dogs.

"Just bring your dress to my room," Chelsea was saying on the phone now as the bright morning sunlight streamed through the windows. "We're all getting ready together. But be here in like three seconds, or Rex's mom is gonna blow her perfectly styled head off." This last part was whispered, and I felt a twinge of guilt for being so uninvolved in helping Chelsea get ready for her wedding.

December had been crazy, though. Between nursing a broken heart and opening a second store at the beginning of the month, and then doing my best to accept the ridiculous happiness that was my life through the second half, I'd been a little busy.

I hung up and turned to face Zane, who was still sprawled in the bed, the covers tucked over his middle while miles of inked golden skin tempted me back to him.

"Is she as stressed as you predicted?" he asked.

"I think so," I told him.

"I'm under strict orders to get to her room right now."

"You should go," he said, his voice still sleepy.

I climbed across the expanse of the king bed and dropped myself onto his chest, breathing in the leather and wood scent of him. "How do you always smell like an Old Fashioned?" I asked him.

"A mystery that might never be solved..."

I wanted to stay with him. But Chelsea needed me, so I climbed a little higher, dropped a long leisurely kiss on his full lips, and then forced myself to slip out of his embrace.

"What time do I have to be where?" he asked.

"Not totally sure," I said. "I'll text you the details when Mrs. Buchanan drills them into me."

"Or maybe they're somewhere in the complex itinerary she left for us," he suggested, pointing at the three-ring binder that had met us when we'd arrived.

"Probably."

"Okay. See you down there."

"Love you," I told him, a little shimmy happening inside me at the freedom I felt when I said those words aloud.

"Love you back."

I grabbed my dress and scooted out of the room to have my hair and makeup done with all the other bridesmaids in Chelsea's suite.

175

# Epilogue - The Wedding Pt. 2
## Zane

As soon as Sabrina was gone, I slipped out of bed. I had things to do today.

It took me about fifteen minutes to shower and dress, and then I was out on the street, breathing in that peculiar musty-fresh scent that I'd only ever smelled in New York City.

I headed down Fifth Avenue, glancing at my phone. I was going to be a few minutes early for the appointment I'd scheduled, so I took my time strolling by the ornate shop windows all done up for the holidays.

The air was crisp and cold, and the sun shone gloriously in a bright cerulean sky, and it was hard not to offer over-exuberant grins to everyone I passed. I had become some new version of myself. One that smiled at strangers.

I chuckled aloud, thinking about the many ways my life had changed recently. As I ducked into a corner bodega to grab a cup of coffee, I replayed the last few months in my head. I didn't miss Denver, not really. The thing was, I really had liked it there. But when John had offered to buy me out of the shop and Rebecca asked if I might consider selling the loft, I didn't even have to think about my answer. I'd already planned to return to

Holly Creek, and those offers seemed to be the universe confirming that I'd made the right decision.

Besides that monetary serendipity, my heart made it crystal clear where I belonged. And as long as Sabrina agreed, my place was with her.

And that was the business I was attending to this morning.

Coffee in hand, I approached the gleaming windows of the jewelry shop. My heart picked up a quicker rhythm as I gazed through the plate glass at the array of sparkling rings and pendants behind the window. Some of the diamonds on display were enormous. Big enough to be gaudy, even, but I wondered if that opinion came from my total inability to afford such a robust declaration of affection.

I stepped through the heavy door, realizing too late that maybe I shouldn't bring my coffee inside. Fancy jewelry shops were not something I had tons of experience with.

"Mr. Crosby?" A woman in a dark suit with a pencil skirt stepped out from behind a near counter to greet me.

"Yes, hi," I said. "Do you want me to..." I held up the coffee cup.

"Oh no, that's fine," she said. "I'm Jill. Would you like to come have a seat and we'll chat a little bit before we get started looking?"

"Sure," I agreed, having no idea how this type of thing normally went.

Jill guided me to a far corner of the shop and we sat, her across a little table from where I was positioned.

"So," she started. "Tell me about Sabrina."

I'd mentioned Sabrina's name on the phone when I'd made the appointment, I guessed, though I didn't remember doing so.

I opened my mouth to answer, but Jill interrupted. "Before you even speak, I just want you to know that the second I said her name, your eyes lit up and your face took on this incredible glow. It makes me so happy to see. That's why I love my job."

I laughed lightly. I had no idea I was so transparent. "She's pretty incredible."

"She must be."

"She owns a couple coffee shops up in Holly Creek, where we live."

"I know the town. Christmas all year round?"

"Practically. They have a huge festival in July and then seem to just leave up the decorations until January."

"That's awesome. And did you guys meet there?"

I ended up talking with Jill for the better part of a half hour, telling her everything about how I met Sabrina, and even getting into some of the years I spent in Holly Creek before I'd ever known her. Jill knew us both pretty well by the time I was done talking, and I guessed that was the point.

"Do you have a photo?" she asked.

"I have lots." I showed her some of my favorite pictures of Sabrina, and Jill gazed at them intently.

"Okay," she said. "I have a few thoughts. Give me a minute."

She wandered the perimeter of the store, gathering rings onto a velvet tray, and then returned, placing the tray on the table where I sat. She talked me through each ring she'd chosen, and I was shocked at how easily I could see any of them on Sabrina's hand. She didn't bother with any of the exceptionally large solitaires, as if even she knew Sabrina wasn't that kind of woman (or maybe, since Jill knew my budget, there was no point in showing me those anyway.)

"They're all incredible," I told her. "But this one is different. This is nuts, but I almost feel like it shines a little more, or there's just something about that I connect with."

"The antique setting. I wondered if you'd gravitate to that one."

I picked up the ring, turning it gingerly in my hand. "It's incredible."

"Do you think that's the one?" Jill asked. She didn't push or pressure, and it felt like she was in this with me, one hundred percent on my side.

"This is the one."

"Let's get you all settled then!" Jill sprang up, leaving me with the ring I'd chosen and moving the tray away. She returned with a tablet, and processed the transaction.

As I left the shop, a tiny square box in my pocket, New York City seemed to slant toward the Plaza Hotel, tipping gently to hurry me on my way back to the woman I loved.

I didn't see Sabrina before the ceremony began. I dressed in our room and then went down, the little box hard against my ribs inside my coat. I wasn't sure I'd even bring it out again this weekend, but I wanted to be prepared, and something about feeling it there just reminded me of the happiness and certainty I felt about this woman, this life.

The groomsmen all loitered around the entrance to the church, which was just down the block from the hotel. As I mounted the steps, one of them greeted me. "Bride or groom?"

"Bride," I answered, feeling a little bit like I was crashing a stranger's wedding. I didn't technically know the bride or the groom.

I was shown to a pew and found a seat toward the center of the church. Soft music played and that strange atmosphere of quiet expectation that I'd only ever known at weddings filled the air. Soon, the music shifted, and the congregants shifted to look back toward the doors, where we could see the bridesmaids and groomsmen in the doorway.

One by one, the couples made their way down the aisle, and when Sabrina appeared, my heart stilled inside me for a long moment. She looked ethereal, her makeup a little heavier than I was used to, but it was sexy as hell. The green satin sheath she wore was fitted, accenting every glorious curve of her body, showcasing her creamy skin. She was like a goddess, and when those bright eyes found me, I felt like the one human man lucky enough to have captured her attention.

The bride was gorgeous too, of course, but through the entire ceremony, my attention was on Sabrina.

When it was over, it felt like years that I lingered in the reception venue alone, nursing a gin and tonic as we waited for the wedding party to appear. She'd warned me that there would be excessive photos required, and she'd clearly been right.

But as I sat at the table where my name appeared on a tiny card next to hers, waiting, my heart was full. I knew this was everything I wanted—not a wedding at the Plaza—but her. Us. And when a slim cool hand dropped onto my shoulder, and I felt Sabrina's breath in my ear, happiness flooded me like sunshine.

"Is this seat taken?" she asked.

I turned to smile up at her and pulled out the chair. "How did everything go?"

She sank into the chair beside me with a sigh. "It was...a lot. But I think Chelsea and Rex are really happy together. It was good."

I'd just returned from the bar with a drink for Sabrina when the bride and groom were announced. The doors opened, and they stepped in, and then the party began in earnest. There were numerous toasts throughout the extensive meal, and it felt like it went on for hours. Because it actually did.

When the cake had been cut, and the DJ had come in to replace the band, and Sabrina and I had spent enough time on the dance floor that no one would call us out for not joining, I took her hands in mine and pulled her close.

"What do you think?" I asked her.

"I'm weddinged out," she laughed. "Think we can sneak away?"

My heart drummed in my chest, suddenly feeling as hard and solid as the little box in my coat pocket. "Yeah," I managed, nerves beginning to spring to life inside me.

"I just need to grab my coat on the way up," Sabrina said, and I followed her out to the coat check in the lobby.

When we stepped in the quiet privacy of the elevator, I pulled her into my arms. I wasn't going to think about what would happen upstairs, the question I wanted to ask her. For this moment, I was going to be right here. Sabrina in my arms, all the love I never knew I could feel in my heart, and everything I needed in the world right here with me.

"I love you so much," I told her.

And she looked up at me with the bright blue eyes that slayed me every time. "I love you too. You're the best thing that's ever happened to me."

I raised my eyes for a second, the eye contact almost too much to bear. And that was when I noticed the sprig of mistletoe hanging over our heads at the top of the elevator. I'd never cared much about holidays... until now.

I kissed Sabrina softly, holding her against me tightly. "Merry Christmas."

She laced her fingers through mine, smiled up at me, and then stepped away, pulling me out of the elevator and toward the rest of our lives together.

Want to find out what happens with that box in Zane's pocket?

Grab the bonus scene at

https://bettingonchristmas.substack.com/

and don't miss the next book in the Betting on Christmas Series at https://books.bookfunnel.com/bettingonchristmas

# Series List - Betting on Christmas

Betting on Christmas Collection Prequel

It Happened One Christmas by Zee Irwin

Mr. Grumpy's Christmas Date by Cat Johnson

Who Needs a Boyfriend at Christmas by Delancey Stewart

He's Looking Like a Christmas Miracle by Amy Stephens

Christmas and Other Inconveniences by Tracy Broemmer

The Christmas Bargain by Peggy McKenzie

Merry & Bright Christmas by Megan Ryder

She's a Hot Christmas Mess by Sofia Alves

Christmas with her Fake Boyfriend by Kim Law

All I Want for Christmas is Her by Harper Cross

Get all the books here:

Scan Me !

# Also by Delancey Stewart

Want more? Get early releases, sneak peeks and freebies! Join my mailing list at www.delanceystewart.com or scan the QR code and get a free story!

### The Zamboni Diaries Series:

*Checking the Center*

*The Wedding Winger*

*Grumpy Goalie*

### The Kasper Ridge Series:

*Only a Summer*

*Only a Fling*

*Only a Crush*

*Only a Secret*

*Only a Touch*

**The Singletree Series:**

*Happily Ever His*

*Happily Ever Hers*

*Shaking the Sleigh*

*Second Chance Spring*

*Falling Into Forever*

*Singletree Box Set 1*

*Singletree Box Set 2*

**The Digital Dating Series (with Marika Ray):**

*Texting with the Enemy*

*While You Were Texting*

*Save the Last Text*

*How to Lose a Girl in 10 Texts*

*The Text Before Christmas*

**The MR. MATCH Series:**

*Prequel: Scoring a Soulmate*

*Book One: Scoring the Keeper's Sister*

*Book Two: Scoring a Fake Fiancée*

*Book Three: Scoring a Prince*

*Book Four: Scoring with the Boss*

*Book Five: Scoring a Holiday Match*

*Mr. Match: The Boxed Set*

**The KINGS GROVE Series:**

*When We Let Go*

*Open Your Eyes*

*When We Fall*

*Open Your Heart*

*Christmas in Kings Grove*

**The STARR RANCH WINERY Series:**

*Chasing a Starr*

**THE GIRLFRIENDS OF GOTHAM Series:**

*Men and Martinis*

*Highballs in the Hamptons*

*Cosmos and Commitment*

*The Girlfriends of Gotham Box Set*

**STANDALONES:**

*Let it Snow*

*Without Words*

*Without Promises*

*Mr. Big*

*Adagio*

**The PROHIBITED! Duet:**

*Prohibited!*

*The Glittering Life of Evie Mckenzie*